D0970399

WANTED

WANTED IS PUBLISHED IN THE UNITED STATES IN 2015 BY SWITCH PRESS
A CAPSTONE IMPRINT
1710 ROE CREST DRIVE
NORTH MANKATO, MINNESOTA 56003
WWW.SWITCHPRESS.COM

TEXT © HOTHOUSE FICTION LTD 2015
SERIES CREATED BY HOTHOUSE FICTION
WWW.HOTHOUSEFICTION.COM

LIBRARY OF CONGRESS CATALOGING-IN-PUBLICATION DATA IS AVAILABLE
ON THE LIBRARY OF CONGRESS WEBSITE.

ISBN: 978-1-63079-007-3 (PAPER OVER BOARD)
ISBN: 978-1-63079-032-5 (EBOOK PDF)
ISBN: 978-1-63079-035-6 (REFLOWABLE EPUB)

SUMMARY: GRACE MILTON HAS ONLY ONE GOAL: BRING THE GUILTLESS
GANG, THE OUTLAWS WHO SLAUGHTERED HER FAMILY, TO JUSTICE.
THAT'S WHY SHE HAD TO ABANDON JOE. SHE COULDN'T AFFORD ANY
DISTRACTIONS. NOW SHE'S MAKING HER LIVING AS ONE OF THE ONLY
FEMALE BOUNTY HUNTERS IN THE WILD WEST, DESPITE THE DOUBTS AND
PROTESTS OF OTHERS. BUT SOON RUMORS SURFACE THAT TWO MEMBERS OF
THE GUILTLESS GANG ARE NEARBY, PLANNING A DARING TRAIN ROBBERY,
AND NOW GRACE IS FACED WITH AN IMPOSSIBLE CHOICE.

DESIGNER: K. FRASER

PHOTO CREDITS: SHUTTERSTOCK

WITH SPECIAL THANKS TO LAURIE J. EDWARDS

PRINTED IN CHINA.
032015   008865RRDF15

Her
COLD
REVENGE

BY ERIN JOHNSON

SWITCH PRESS

Grace Milton, a young woman living in the Arizona Territory, watches as her family is killed by the ruthless men known as the Guiltless Gang. Her house and former life are destroyed in a merciless fire.

Grace makes a promise to herself. She will hunt down every member of the Guiltless Gang no matter what it takes. Even if it makes her as hard and ruthless as her enemies. Grace becomes a bounty hunter, meeting fear, disbelief and scorn along the way. Then she meets a handsome young drifter named Joe. Joe lost his own family years ago and can feel the pain in Grace's heart. As the man's kindness begins to grow into something more, Grace is torn. If she opens her heart will she be strong enough to finish her quest? **Will loving this dark-haired stranger turn her aside from reaping her cold revenge?**

CHAPTER 1

In the flickering candlelight of her cramped room, Grace studied the wanted posters she had draped over the washstand and the chair and tacked against the wall. Not that she needed to. Every detail of the faces of her family's killers had been burned into her mind. She had memorized each feature, each scar, the hard look in each eye, and the twist of each sneer. Yet even then she couldn't help staring at the shadows flitting back and forth across the images of the Guiltless Gang, making them appear even more sinister. Desire for revenge smoldered like a constant flame inside her, burning around her heart. Yet in the weeks since Grace had left Tombstone and arrived in Bisbee, not a whisper of their whereabouts had circulated. Not one clue had made its way into the gossip floating around town, and she had no idea where the gang was holed up. Last she'd heard they'd fled like the cowards they were. It was as if they'd completely disappeared. One thing was certain — if she got even an inkling of where to find any one of them, she wouldn't hesitate to hunt them down.

Stretching out on her narrow bed in the tiny attic room, Grace swallowed bitterly at her thoughts. Below her, the cacophony in the saloon swelled, the boasts and laughter growing more raucous, chasing off sleep and underscoring her loneliness. The ache of loss and regret spiraled up, reminding her how isolated she was, and how unprotected. Her hand snaked out and curved around her father's revolver, tucked under her pillow, and more memories fed painfully into her mind. Pa had taught her and Daniel to shoot, to protect themselves from the dangers of the desert — rattlesnakes, slinking coyotes, rabid animals. He'd never expected to be ambushed by humans . . .

Nightmares of the past closed around her. She was back in the root cellar, peering through the tiny slit, helpless while the Guiltless Gang slaughtered her family one by one. Ma crumpled on the ground, tiny Abby beside her, and her brother Daniel too. Pa's eyes had warned her to be still, to save baby Zeke, before a murderous bullet took him too. Then as her family's cabin burned, Grace had fought her way through smoke that clogged her lungs, constricted her breathing, desperate with hope.

But it was no use. Zeke's small body lay in her arms, lifeless . . .

With the palms of her hands, Grace pressed away the tears that began to roll down the sides of her face, and the horror of the memory dimmed — though it would never fully disappear. The candle burning low on the table beside her came into focus, and she rolled over and snuffed the flame, then lay rigid in the darkness as the bangs and shouts downstairs intensified. The scuffling and shouting crescendoed into crashes, curses, and threats, and soon she heard the saloon doors bang open, followed by screams and gunshots.

Her hand tightened on the Colt's grip. Yes, Pa had trained her to kill wild animals, but did outlaws fit that description? Would Pa ever have believed his daughter capable of killing a man? She squeezed her eyes shut, and there was Guiltless member Doc Slaughter, pinning a helpless girl against the hay bales in a dark alley. Grace had acted on instinct to save that girl — and, if she was honest, to avenge the murder of her brother Daniel. But could she do it again if she faced another of those criminals? In a way, she was more worried she might never get the chance.

Although she'd marched through the crowd at the Bird Cage Theater and declared herself a bounty hunter, she was now alone and near penniless and beginning to doubt her choice. The reward money she'd received for killing Slaughter had seemed a fortune, but after a few months without much work, the money in her pouch had dwindled to almost nothing. And the townspeople made it clear they weren't likely to hire a sixteen-year-old female to track down criminals. If she didn't get work tomorrow, she'd find herself on the street.

She considered returning to the Ndeh tribe who had shown her such kindness, but that would mean facing Joe. Grace knew she wouldn't be able to look him in the eye; she wouldn't be able to explain why she'd left without him after the kiss they'd shared. Too afraid to love someone after everything that had happened to her, and fearful love would keep her from her mission, she'd bolted. Still, in spite of herself, most nights she relived each moment they'd shared . . . but tonight she couldn't — wouldn't — think of Joe. Memories of him only brought more pain.

Suddenly, Grace heard heavy boots stomping up the stairs.

Her fist clutched at the covers. She'd paid extra for this tiny attic room with its smelly mattress and its bugs and mice that crawled over her in the dark, because the room's location offered a bit more protection. Few people climbed the stairs — until now. She listened hard. She knew her rent was overdue, but those boots clunking up the stairs weren't her landlady's. Had Miz Bessie sent someone to throw her out?

Grace's muscles stiffened as the doorknob rattled, but though it twisted and turned, the lock didn't give way.

A loud, angry exhale was followed by fists banging the wood so hard the center panel bowed inward, and she knew the flimsy door couldn't withstand more pounding. Miz Bessie would blame her if the wood shattered, and she had no money to pay the rent, let alone replace the door.

Clutching her revolver, Grace slipped out of bed and flicked open the lock, then stood to one side, gun aimed, as she yanked open the shuddering door.

CHAPTER 2

A man, his fist up to pound the door again, pitched forward
into Grace's room. He staggered a few steps and then
clutched at the washstand to steady himself. Grace wheeled
around to keep the gun pointed at his chest. Moonlight
glinting through her small window illuminated the hard
planes of the stranger's face and the jagged scar that ran
from the edge of his mouth to his eyebrow, pulling one
side of his mouth into a permanent smirk. She took an
involuntary step back as his startled expression changed to
a glower.

"What ya doing in my room?"

His slurred words and his eyes, glazed and unfo-
cused, revealed the long hours spent in the bar below.

Grace straightened to her full height, but the man still towered over her, his body leaning forward menacingly.

"You're mistaken. This is my room." Grace spat out each word, but she couldn't contain her trembling. Had Miz Bessie rented out this room to him? Or worse yet, made good on her threat to make Grace service paying customers?

The man's small bleary eyes conveyed his confusion. "I pay — *hic* — paid for thish." He shook his head. "Room at top of stairs."

No, it couldn't be. She had begged Miz Bessie for a little time.

A gleam lit the man's eye. "Musta paid for more than I thought. Come 'ere, lil darling." He staggered toward her, teeth bared in a jagged, mirthless grin.

Grace backed up until she bumped into the bed.

"That's it, girlie. You and me gonna have us some fun."

She stepped away from the bed, setting her jaw and berating herself for retreating. She gestured at him with the revolver. "Stay back."

The man halted, swaying back and forth. His uncomprehending eyes fixed on the Colt. He blinked several times. "That ain't what I think it is?"

Grace's teeth clenched so tightly she could barely force out the words. "I'm not afraid to use this." She dipped the revolver low enough to make the color leave his face, then moved her aim back up to his heart.

His low, throaty chuckle ended in a sneer. "Lil thing like you don't know how to use that."

Grace pitched her voice as deep and menacing as she could. "Get out."

The man stumbled to one side, but steadied himself again on the washstand. "Not before I get wh-what's on offer," he slurred, lunging toward her.

She sidestepped smoothly, and the drunkard crashed face first onto the wooden floor planks. She kept her gun trained on him as he lay in a heap, his breath coming in uneven gasps, but when he remained motionless, Grace nudged him with her foot. No response, no groan. He was out cold. She squatted beside him, uncertain what to do. She could try to drag him into the hall, but what if he woke and wanted revenge? Or worse yet, what if he was one of Miz Bessie's customers? In that case, she'd best leave now and not come back until she could pay her debts and then some. Miz Bessie would forgive anything if Grace waved enough money in front of her.

She gathered her belongings from the drawers, stuffing them into the saddlebag, and then collected her rope and the bow and arrows the Ndeh tribe had given her. She stepped gingerly over the man and headed out, feeling her way in the darkness as she crept down the back staircase. A few lamps still burned in the narrow hall and along the second set of stairs, making her descent easier, but she tripped on a loose carpet runner on the lower landing and barely managed to catch herself before she crashed into the door at the bottom of the steps. Turning the knob, she eased the door open a little and peered into the saloon. A few patrons were still hunched over the bar, backs to her, and close by two cowboys slumped over a table, too groggy to notice her. Grace waited until the barman turned to refill a glass, then tiptoed to the rear exit and slipped out into the darkness.

She crept along the alley, making sure to keep to the shadows, her gun clutched tightly in her hand. Traveling alone at this time of night was dangerous, but not as dangerous as staying in her attic room with that lecherous stranger. She had to head out of town. Her stay with the Ndeh had taught her survival and tracking skills, and in many ways she felt safer out in the desert or the mountains. But there was something she needed first.

When she reached the stable, she had to bang several times before the doors creaked open and a bleary-eyed stable hand stared out at her.

"I'm here for my horse." He didn't respond or pull the gates wide enough for her to enter until Grace added, "Bullet." Then it seemed he couldn't open up quickly enough.

She hadn't found a stable yet that could handle her high-spirited palomino. Bullet responded only to her — she'd roped him as a wild colt and broken him herself. Even Pa had given Bullet a wide berth . . . At another thought of him, Grace's throat closed and she blinked to clear the mist from her eyes. Not now. She'd think of her father again when she could grieve him properly.

"Bullet?" Grace called into the cavernous blackness that reeked of manure, trampled straw, and old horse blankets. The racket in a far stall ceased, and when her eyes adjusted to the gloom, Grace headed toward the nickering palomino, whispering calming words as she passed stalls filled with snorting and stamping horses.

When she reached Bullet's stall, she struggled to undo the latch and noticed a section of his door was bowing out. He must have been kicking at the wood again. She'd already paid to replace the stall door twice. Grace rubbed his nose and sighed. Bullet had been so happy at the Ndeh camp — if only they *could* go back to the warmth and closeness of the Indian village. But she once again reminded herself that Joe might still be with them, and she couldn't afford any distractions. She had to concentrate on her mission: tracking down her family's killers and bringing them to justice.

A short while later, she and Bullet streaked down the road toward Tombstone. They both loved cantering down the deserted trail, braids and mane blowing in the cool night air. Grace kept one hand on the pistol holstered at her side; the other hand held the reins loosely, giving Bullet his head. The horse needed his freedom after being corralled for so long, and the beauty of the stars twinkling overhead tempted her to relax and enjoy the scenery, but she knew she had to remain alert for the desert's many dangers. Soon grayness smudged the sky to the east, followed by streaks of yellow and pink along the horizon. As they traveled on, Grace patted her rawhide containers again to be sure they were full of water. Ever since the stable hands in Tombstone had sabotaged her water bags, she always checked and rechecked her supply. Once the sun rose, the heat shimmering on the desert clay and sand would quickly cause dehydration, so she pulled Bullet to a halt and gave him a drink. One thing she had learned was that you could never be too cautious.

By early morning, they reached the outskirts of Tombstone, and Grace headed straight for the sheriff's office in the courthouse. Sheriff Behan had been away on "family business" ever since Grace had received the reward money for killing Doc Slaughter; the Guiltless Gang had been paying Behan for protection, and the sheriff failed to deliver. In Behan's absence, Deputy Clayton had captured many crooks, but had apparently seen neither hide nor hair of the Guiltless Gang. Even if it wasn't a priority for the law, Grace would never abandon her hunt for those murderers. But for now she would hunt whatever petty criminals appeared on the new wanted posters so she could pay Miz Bessie. Dismounting, she tied Bullet's reins to a hitching post outside the courthouse, frowning as he snorted and nosed her arm.

"Please," she whispered. "Stay calm until I come out."

She and Bullet had already made enough enemies in this town; they did not need any more. She ran a soothing hand down Bullet's neck, and then turned and strode quickly toward the courthouse. Behind her, Bullet stamped and tossed his head, but at least he didn't rear.

Inside the sheriff's office, Deputy Clayton sat at the smaller of the two desks. The other desk remained empty, and Grace pursed her lips at Behan's continued cowardice. The deputy looked up when she entered.

"Can I help —?" He squinted at her. "Oh, Miss Milton, it's you."

He stood and motioned her to a hard-backed chair, and she sat on the edge of the seat and leaned forward.

"I came to see about more bounty work."

Clayton cleared his throat, averting his eyes. When he spoke, his syrupy, patronizing tone seemed geared to pacify a young child whose sticky sweet had fallen into the dirt. "Well now, you know how much we appreciate what you did at the Bird Cage Theater. Ridding us of a notorious criminal and all. Very admirable."

"And . . . ?" Grace prompted after he paused.

The deputy tilted back his chair, gazed at the ceiling, and stroked his chin. "Thing is, most people don't abide by a woman chasing outlaws."

Grace gripped the chair arms and struggled to keep her temper in check.

The deputy drawled on. "The men round these parts just don't like being shown up by a girl. And you got to consider that some of 'em have families to feed."

"I need to eat too."

Deputy Clayton tendered an apologetic smile and sighed. "A pretty girl like you should just get yourself a husband."

He looked at her sincerely, but Grace almost choked. She hid her clenched fists under the folds of her calico skirt, but she couldn't keep the tartness from her words. "I have something important to do first."

Deputy Clayton's eyes filled with pity. "That's no life for a woman."

Grace wished she hadn't made public her plan to bring every member of the Guiltless Gang to justice. The deputy had done everything he could to discourage her — maybe he even knew the gang's whereabouts. Was he keeping it from her so other bounty hunters could capture them?

"If you need money, I hear old Miss Billings needs a seamstress . . ." he ventured.

Grace suppressed a sigh and shook her head.

"Miss Billings is a mite testy at times, but she'd pay you well."

"I'm no good with a needle and thread." Grace bit out the words. Pa had needed her help breaking the horses, so she'd never even learned to sew.

The deputy's eyebrows drew together. "Well, what about housekeeping? I could ask around."

Grace stared hard at him, unwavering.

When the silence dragged on, Deputy Clayton sighed. "Fine. All's I have are a few cold cases or petty criminals." He waved a hand at the wall of wanted posters.

"Which ones are they?"

"Not worth the time, if you ask me."

She hadn't asked him. *He* didn't have rent overdue and only a handful of pemmican for the next few meals. Grace would take whatever she could get. She strode over to the wall and, turning to him, she asked again. "Which ones?"

Clayton pointed toward the three smaller posters in the bottom row with tiny, hand-drawn pictures. "That one on the right just came in yesterday."

Chaney Grewell. Grace could hardly make out the man's face, and the bounty was a pittance. At first his features didn't look familiar, but she tilted the poster until sunlight fell across the rough sketch. One thing stood out — a scar from eyebrow to lip. She frowned. That very man had been lying at her feet out cold, and she'd stepped over him. If she'd known, she would have tied him up and brought him along to Tombstone. She could have claimed the bounty money here and now — it was true that the reward was small, but it would pay a few weeks' rent.

She turned and rushed toward the door. "I'll be back," she called over her shoulder.

After giving Bullet some water and taking a swig herself, she swung into the saddle. Most likely Grewell had
already left Bisbee, but if she returned before the trail went
cold, she could track him down. The Ndeh had taught her
well, and surely someone at the saloon would know which
way he'd gone. She was tired, having ridden all night, but
there was no time to rest now.

The trip back to Bisbee in the hot sun took longer
than the early morning ride, but Grace curbed her impatience and stopped for water so that neither she nor Bullet
collapsed from the heat. After the hot, sweaty ride through
the desert, she finally guided Bullet toward the shade
of the stable. As soon as he was settled, she would go after
her quarry.

But as she arrived, the stable hand crossed his arms and
blocked the entrance. "You didn't pay your bill."

"I just got a job, and I'll be paying Miz Bessie shortly."

A dubious look crossed the boy's face.

"I promise. I'll be back with money," she said earnestly
as the stable hand deliberated. Every minute she wasted
here gave her bounty time to get away.

Finally the boy stepped aside to let her by. "You best be
telling the truth." When Bullet passed him, he flattened
himself against the opposite stall. "Thought we were rid of
that devil for good," he muttered.

Grace led Bullet to the stall with the bowed door.
The palomino balked, but when she entered the stall first

the horse followed, and she gave him a hasty rubdown and some feed, all the time worried that the man she was after might be long gone. As soon as she was done, she hurried over to the saloon.

Grace hesitated when she saw Miz Bessie standing at the counter — she'd hoped to avoid her until she had the reward money, but Bessie caught sight of her and marched over, hand outstretched.

"Oh no you don't, missy. No room unless you pay. You already owe me for the past week."

"Miz Bessie, I have a job. I'll be getting paid for it, possibly even today. I promise I'll pay you as soon as I get the money."

The landlady wagged her finger in Grace's face. "If that money isn't in my hand tomorrow, don't even think about coming back here."

"I'll pay."

The older woman growled something, then turned and stalked toward the bar.

First, Grace had to find Grewell. Miz Bessie might know his whereabouts, but Grace was reluctant to ask. It didn't sound as if Bessie'd had anything to do with him showing up at her room, but if Grewell had broadcast the story of what happened last night and Miz Bessie figured out who did it, she might turn her out for good. But it was her only chance at a lead, so she had to take the risk. She hesitantly walked over to the heavyset lady.

"Um, Miz Bessie, have you seen a man with a scar around here this morning . . . ?"

"Lotsa men round here got scars," she replied, not bothering to look up.

"This one has a scar from his eyebrow to his mouth —"

Miz Bessie glanced up sharply. "You best not get mixed up with someone like that."

"I didn't mean . . ." Grace's voice trailed off. "I just wondered," she finished lamely.

"Stay away from him." The sharpness in Miz Bessie's voice was tempered by a note of concern that surprised Grace. She bit her lip and decided to try another tack.

"I intend to. That's why I wondered if he was still around," she said.

"Mmhmm. Well, he slunk down those stairs — or should I say crawled down 'em — early this morning. Never did say how he got that bloody nose or those bruises on his face."

Some of the tension eased from Grace's shoulders. Grewell hadn't made mention of her — no doubt he didn't want to admit he'd been outsmarted by a girl. Miz Bessie tilted her chin.

"Told him I don't abide by fighting in this establishment. Told him to find another place to stay." She sniffed. "He tried to sneak out without paying for his drinks. I sent him packing."

"Do you know where he went?"

"I expect he headed to *that* saloon down the street," she replied, screwing up her face. She never said the name of her fiercest competitor. "That man's trouble if I ever seen it."

"I don't want anything to do with him." *Except to capture him.*

Now that she had an idea where the man might have gone, Grace was eager to chase him down, but she didn't want Miz Bessie to suspect she was after him. With the way that the landlady gossiped, word would spread quickly, and Grace didn't want her quarry to know she was pursuing him.

Rather than going out the front door, she went back to the stable. Miz Bessie might be right about him heading to the rival saloon, but checking if he'd moved his horse to another stable would be a quick way to get another lead.

The stable hand raised an eyebrow when she appeared in the doorway. "Back already? Got that money so soon, huh?"

"Not just yet," she said impatiently. "I need to find a man named Grewell. He has a scar down his face." She indicated on her own face with her hand. "You know if his horse is stabled here?"

The boy directed a savage glance in Bullet's direction. "I can't think about no other horses when that beast's making such a racket."

She strode back to Bullet's stall and calmed him, then

marched back toward the stable hand. "The faster I find him, the faster you get paid."

"He owe you money?"

Grace gritted her teeth. The stable hand was proving even less helpful than Miz Bessie. Grewell could be halfway to Tucson by now. "Is his horse here or not?" Irritation sharpened her words, and the stable hand frowned.

"Don't get so testy," he retorted, then jerked a thumb toward a nearby pinto. Grace sighed with relief. Grewell hadn't left town yet, but who knew how long he'd stay? She needed that money, and she needed it now — she couldn't give him a chance to slip away from her. Moving quickly along Main Street, she looked in at one saloon after another, but there was no sign of him. A man with a scar like that wouldn't easily go unnoticed, so she guessed he must be keeping out of sight.

About to turn the corner to search the back alleys, Grace doubled back as she suddenly spotted her prey. He was skulking outside the general store, keeping to the darker corners. Her breathing quickened with excitement. All she had to do was catch him, and the bounty would be hers. She watched as Grewell slid into the alley beside the store and pulled out his tobacco pouch, inserting a pinch into his mouth and slouching against the wooden planks of the building. Even from this distance, his battered and swollen face looked painful, and he winced as he chewed.

Grace pressed her body against a nearby wall and then stealthily moved closer so she could observe him more closely. But before she got near enough to surprise him, he straightened and walked back toward Main Street. Grace followed, ready to return to the shadows if he turned. Grewell seemed quite brazen now, striding down the street and even tipping his hat to the sheriff, although he angled his head away and pretended to stroke that side of his face, so his hand hid the scar. As the sheriff nodded and strolled past, she wanted to shout that he was nodding good day to a criminal, but it was just as well. She'd capture the man herself, and then turn him in for that reward money.

After trailing him to the stable, Grace slipped into the dark building and ducked behind stacked bales of hay. She wished she were near enough to get the rope hanging on Bullet's saddle and restrain the man without firepower. If she pulled a gun on Grewell, he might shoot and injure horses or innocent people. She watched, frustrated, as Grewell passed her hiding place, leading his pinto into the courtyard. She followed silently, trying to quiet her breathing. All she had to do was slip up behind him, slide her hand into his holster, and hold him at gunpoint with his own revolver. Many times she'd watched Ndeh warriors use this technique to catch their enemies by surprise. No one ever heard them coming.

Ever so cautiously, she moved up behind him and snaked out her hand . . .

In front of them, a rat darted from a hole in the stable wall, and the pinto reared. Grewell jumped back, knocking straight into Grace as she sneaked up behind him. She tumbled to the ground, her gun arm pinned under her.

Grewell wheeled around, and his eyes widened. "What the . . . you?"

Before Grace could untangle herself from her skirts or reach her gun, Grewell swung himself onto his horse's back and galloped off, cursing under his breath.

CHAPTER 3

Grace threw the saddle on her own still-sweating horse, and then slung her bow and quiver of arrows over her shoulder, hitched her lasso to the saddle horn, and led Bullet quickly from the stable. She mounted him in one swift motion and set off at a gallop toward the puffs of dust rising rapidly in the distance.

"Go, Bullet, go," she urged. All she needed was to get within roping distance . . .

Bullet soon closed the distance between them and Grewell, and as they neared him she unholstered her Colt, holding on to her reins with one hand. With her skills, he was an easy target. She was sure she could get her man without even wounding him or his horse. It was all in the aim. Squeezing off a shot, she allowed herself a small congratulatory smile as the bullet whistled right past his horse's ear. Exactly what she'd planned.

The pinto bucked, spilling Grewell to the ground, and he lay dazed for a few seconds, then crawled to his knees, rubbing his lower back and struggling to stand. As soon as he got to his feet, Grace twirled her lasso and let it fly. She'd been roping wild horses since she was ten, so her aim was true — the lasso dropped straight over Grewell's head and fell around his waist. Just at the right moment, she yanked hard, pulling the rope taut and imprisoning his arms below the elbows. With another hard tug, she yanked him clean off his feet. He cried out in confusion and surprise, and she dragged the kicking, yelling man a few feet. She kept a tight hold on the rope, looping it up as she galloped closer and jerking the rope to knock him off his feet whenever he attempted to stand.

His face contorted with fury, Grewell gazed up at Grace as she pulled Bullet to a halt beside him. "Believe you're a wanted man, Mr. Grewell," she called down to him.

Squinting in the bright sunlight, he glared at her. Then his face changed. He stared in shock. "A girl?"

Grace smiled down at him and touched the brim of her hat. As he saw her more closely, he did a double-take.

"You're that girl from *last night*!" he almost whimpered. "Wh-what you aim to do to me?"

"Keep still."

Her captive twisted and turned like a freshly caught fish as he floundered on the ground, but the rope kept his arms pinned to his sides. He wriggled his fingers, struggling to reach his gun, but years of dealing with wild horses had given Grace quick reflexes. She dismounted from Bullet and, keeping a tight hold of the rope, went over to Grewell, evading his grasping fingers as she leaned over and plucked his revolver from its holster. Then, pointing it at him, she warned, "You don't cooperate, I'll have no trouble using this." She patted the holster at her side. "Or this." Yanking the trussed man to his feet, she looked him in the eye. "And I'm warning you now. My horse is wild, so I'd advise you to walk carefully beside us or you'll likely get hurt . . . or killed."

Grace couldn't help feeling a celebratory swell of pride in herself as she put a lead rope on Grewell's horse, then remounted. She'd finally made a bounty, her first in weeks. Maybe she was cut out for this after all.

As she nudged Bullet in a slow circle to face toward town, she noticed a cloud of dust rising in the nearby hills. She squinted, unsure what was causing the swirling sand, but her heart began to pound faster as the hazy twister separated into a group of cowboys galloping toward her.

Grace's hand went straight for her gun, and soon four men had reined their horses into a circle around her. Like mirror images with their squinty eyes and tangled red beards, they all stared at her. The Watkins brothers.

Grace had seen them at the saloon, and she knew them each by name and by reputation as some of the most notorious bounty hunters in the West. They traveled north from the Mexican border, nabbing criminals as they went, though some said they were more lawless than the outlaws they captured.

"Well, look here," the middle brother, Asa, sneered. "We got ourselves some bounty, all roped up and ready to deliver."

What? Fury set Grace trembling, but she knew enough about the Watkins brothers to rein in her temper. She sat up straighter, narrowing her eyes and working to keep her voice from wobbling. "This is my capture."

The oldest brother, Frank, stroked his beard. "That so?"

Before she could react, he whipped out his pistol and shot Grewell through his shoulder. His shrieks echoed through the nearby canyon, and Grace struggled to stay in the saddle and keep Bullet under control as his pinto squealed and reared.

"Why'd you do that?" Grace yelled.

"I got my reasons." Frank motioned to his youngest brother, who hopped from his horse and dodged the pinto's crashing hooves. Whipping a knife from his boot, Asa sliced the rope tethering the pinto to Bullet.

"Hey!" she sputtered, so furious she shook harder now.

Asa hung on to the rope and waited for the pinto to stop bucking, then handed it to Frank.

"How dare you! That's my rope and *my* captive!"

Frank spat toward Bullet's hooves. "Is that so? Who you think the law'll believe? You or us?"

"We got ourselves four witnesses . . ." Asa waved an arm toward his brothers.

"And that's my bullet in his shoulder," Frank added. "Maybe you should've shot him when you got the chance." He threw back his head and laughed.

Steven grinned at his brothers, looking for sport now. "That there gun," he said, "ain't no gun for a woman. Who'd you steal it from?"

She glared at him, her hands balled into fists. "It was my father's."

"He should've taught you to shoot it then."

"Oh, I can shoot all right." She'd like to demonstrate by putting a bullet in each one of them, but they had four guns to her one.

Wade shook his head and gave her a doubtful yet sympathetic glance. The other three burst into loud laughter.

Grace gritted her teeth, her gun hand itching to pull the trigger.

"Heard you spent time with some Injuns," Frank taunted, motioning to the bow and arrows on her back. He turned to his brothers. "Wonder what she learned from those squaws." His leer gave Grace chills.

"Don't you dare come near me," she growled, gripping her gun. She'd shoot him if he touched her.

Wade spoke up. "Aw, leave her be. We best head for town and turn in this outlaw before the sheriff closes up for the night, anyway. Bounty ain't much, but it'll buy a round of drinks . . ."

Frank nodded. "Let's go." But he turned to ogle Grace for a few seconds. "You haven't seen the last of us, 'specially if you plan on keeping this up. Bounty hunting ain't no game for ladies."

He smirked, then turned his horse toward town, his brothers following close behind.

She barely even thought about it. As she watched the Watkins brothers' retreating backs, Grace reached behind her and pulled out an arrow. Breathing out her pent-up anger to quell her shaking, she loaded her bow and took aim. Her first arrow pierced Asa's ten-gallon hat, sending it flying. Her second grazed Frank's cheek, enough to sting and set him howling in pain, but not enough to do major damage.

They pulled up their horses, and Frank wheeled his around, still clutching his cheek. "Why you —" he began, drawing his gun and aiming across the distance between them.

"That there is a warning," Grace shouted, her voice quaking again, "not to underestimate me."

"Let's go, Frank," Wade shouted. "Ignore her."

Frank gave her one final glare before they turned their horses again and galloped away. Grace settled her bow back on her shoulder, grinding her teeth. She knew she had the skill to pick off those Watkins brothers one by one if she wanted to, but her conscience wouldn't let her. She'd have no just cause — they were dishonest and corrupt but they'd done nothing more than play dirty with her. Memories of the Ndeh's sense of justice came tumbling into her mind and she reached into Bullet's saddlebag, pulling out the feathered headband Cheis, the Ndeh chief, had given her for saving the tribe's children when they were under attack. One feather was gone — the feather that had fluttered onto Doc Slaughter's lifeless body. Five feathers remained. Until each feather rested on a member of the Guiltless Gang, she would never be free to move on with her life. She'd see that those responsible for murdering her family were brought to justice, no matter how long it took.

That cause, she felt, was just — by any means.

Yet the thought of killing brought back memories of her family and their cruel, senseless murders. Their blood spilled onto the ground, their cabin burned to ashes. Yes, she'd helped the Ndeh tribe fight off the soldiers who'd raided the village; yes, she'd shot Doc Slaughter — however, she'd had no choice then. But she still couldn't help but worry, if she came face to face with another member of the Guiltless Gang, would she be able to pull the trigger?

Grace patted Bullet's neck as disappointment and worry began to overtake her sense of anger. The Watkins brothers had become only specks on the horizon, but as they'd headed toward Tombstone, she decided to set out in the opposite direction. Miz Bessie might agree to one more night in the room at the saloon in Bisbee. After that, Grace had no idea what she'd do.

She needed some bounties — now.

CHAPTER 4

As Grace dejectedly led Bullet into the alley by the stable, someone shouted her name. Few people in town knew it, and those who did either wanted payment or planned to cause trouble. She continued leading the horse, quickening her steps and fixing her gaze straight ahead, pretending she hadn't heard.

"Grace? Grace Milton, wait."

This time she recognized Reverend Byington's voice, with not a little relief. She stopped and turned to him with a smile as the preacher hurried toward her.

"I thought that was you," he said breathlessly, reaching out to stroke Bullet's nose. "And I'd know this gorgeous palomino anywhere."

Bullet snorted and flicked his head, clearly not keen to take the compliment, but when the preacher extended his other hand with a slice of apple on his palm, Bullet gobbled it quick enough and let Reverend Byington pat his neck.

He laughed. "I'd been planning to give that treat to my own horse, but it went to a worthy cause." He focused on Grace. "So you're staying in Bisbee? I wondered why I hadn't seen you in Tombstone for some time."

Grace scuffed the toe of her boot in the dirt. "Yes . . . I, uh . . ." She didn't want to share that her main reason for leaving was to avoid seeing Joe when he came into town for supplies.

The preacher held up his hand.

"Why don't you get your horse settled for the night, then we can meet for dinner at the hotel and you can tell me how you've been?"

Grace hesitated — she had no money for a meal, and even if she had, she couldn't waste it at such a fancy establishment. She'd been planning to eat the few crumbs of pemmican left in her pouch.

"My treat, of course," the preacher added, seeming to sense her hesitation.

"Oh . . . I-I couldn't."

"Nonsense." He waved his hand to brush aside her protests. "I insist."

Although she hated to be beholden to anyone, she

knew she could do with a good meal. Someday, though, she'd find a way to pay back all of Reverend Byington's generosity.

A short while later, Grace sat in the elegant dining room across from the preacher, closing her eyes and inhaling the aromatic steam from a bowl of beef stew. Her stomach growled, but she waited patiently if a little skeptically until Reverend Byington had asked the blessing. Then, finally, she dipped her spoon into the thick, dark broth and savored this bit of heaven.

The balding man with the scruffy gray beard sitting opposite her didn't resemble the angels described in his Bible — and given all that had happened to her, she wasn't sure she believed in such things anymore. But if they did exist, then to Grace, Reverend Byington had been an angel and more. Somehow he always caught her at her lowest times and offered aid. When she'd almost died of dehydration in the desert and he'd come to her aid with water and food. When he'd found the photograph of her family she'd thought was lost forever. And later, when he'd strode into the saloon and championed her cause after she'd shot Doc Slaughter. Now he was feeding her? Sometimes his kindness was overwhelming, but it served as a healing balm, soothing the frustration and fear balled up inside her. Every muscle in her body, taut and alert against sudden attacks, unknotted. Even if she didn't believe the preacher's message, his caring and generosity touched her spirit.

With Reverend Byington's gentle prodding, Grace spilled the whole saga with the Watkins brothers between bites of potatoes, carrots, and chunks of beef.

Reverend Byington frowned. "I'm headed into Tombstone tomorrow. That outlaw you caught knows the truth. Perhaps I can convince him to divulge it."

"He'd admit to being captured by a lone girl rather than four burly men?" She wanted to be polite, but her tone came out a mixture of sarcastic and incredulous.

Reverend Byington smiled a little and stroked his beard. "You may be right. Pride often trumps truth."

"Better to let it go," she said with a sigh. She sure could have used that reward money.

The preacher set his fork on his plate and leaned toward her. "Better yet, leave it to God. Then it's sure to work out for the best."

Grace pinched her lips together to curb the stream of resentment that bubbled up and threatened to erupt. Where was God when that gang stole her family's horses, torched her home, and murdered her parents and siblings? When she dug their grave all night long until her palms were bleeding and blistered? Or, indeed, just this afternoon when she'd lost the bounty she so desperately needed to survive? Did that all work out for the best?

As if the preacher sensed her thoughts, he reached across the table and patted her hand. "Sometimes it's hard to understand God's purpose for allowing tragedies, but rest assured, He does love us," Reverend Byington said, his eyes filled with sympathy.

Grace lowered her gaze and concentrated on corralling bits of onion floating in her stew. She wouldn't argue with him after he had been so generous, but she had a hard time believing God cared for her. She'd seen too much evidence to the contrary.

Reverend Byington's expression shifted to a concerned frown. "So, other than today's fiasco, how have you been? Besides bounty hunting, what have you been doing?"

Grace felt guilty as she realized that he imagined her success in bounty hunting to have been greater than it was. She longed to confide her true situation, but likely the preacher would insist on paying her room and board in addition to tonight's meal, and she couldn't let him do that.

"Not a great deal . . . trying to make a success of this new line of work takes up most of my time." She smiled weakly. "Uh, how have your travels been?"

Reverend Byington frowned at her lack of elaboration, but then his face softened. "Are you missing your Ndeh friends . . . and Joe? I passed the village a week ago, and all seemed well." His jaw tightened. "As well as it can be with the cavalry hunting them down."

Grace drew in a sharp breath. "They weren't attacked again, were they?"

"No, no. I didn't mean to alarm you." The preacher's

sigh came from deep within his chest. "I was referring to the overall state of affairs. Most people don't believe that the good Lord's command to love everyone includes the savages."

"They're not savages," Grace snapped, unable to hide her irritation.

"Perhaps not in my eyes or yours or in God's." With a look of sadness on his face, Reverend Byington gestured around the dining room. "But most people would term them so. It's always a relief to see the Ndeh safe and unharmed."

She nodded, calming down a little. "So everyone was doing well?"

"It seemed so."

"I'm glad." She fidgeted in her chair and tried to keep her voice casual. "And . . . you say Joe was with them?"

The preacher glanced up at her as he wiped his lips with his napkin, pausing for a moment before he spoke again.

"Actually, I ran into Joe in town — Tombstone, that is — a few days ago, buying supplies for the Ndeh. I had a meal with him there, much like we're having here."

Grace stared at the dregs of the beef stew in her bowl. "Did he . . . did he, umm, mention me?"

"Can't say I recall . . ."

Grace hoped the jab of pain to her heart wasn't reflected on her face, but the preacher quickly back-pedaled.

"I'm sure he thinks about you often," he said kindly.

Did Joe really think about her? Or had she broken his heart so badly he put her out of his mind forever? On that last night together, the strength of their passion when they finally kissed could have ignited a starburst . . . but then she'd slipped away before dawn, leaving him behind without so much as a goodbye. She'd been afraid — not only of the intensity of their feelings for each other, but that Joe was the one person who could make her forget her quest for justice. A quest he'd labeled as revenge.

Reverend Byington cleared his throat, startling Grace from her thoughts.

"I must say, I'm glad you're turning your talents to helping the law rather than vengeance."

She cringed. Of course Reverend Byington agreed with Joe. Both of them, and the Ndeh, had urged her to forgive her parents' murderers. She had felt surrounded by people who didn't understand — she could not let those outlaws roam free, destroying lives and property, killing other innocent people.

When she didn't answer, the preacher continued. "To be honest, I'd like to see you find another line of work, though. One more suited to women. The Jones family is still looking for help with the children and household chores . . ."

Grace shook her head, irritation rising in her again. "I have a job to do, Reverend. And I won't rest until it's done.

Doesn't the Good Book say we should use our talents? My talents are tracking, riding, and shooting."

Byington smiled a little. "I really don't think that's what —"

The carved wooden hotel doors burst open. One of the women who worked in the saloon across the street came marching into the dining room, glancing around, until her gaze fell on Grace.

Then she strode straight toward their table.

CHAPTER 5

The woman slapped her hands on the table so hard the china rattled. "You're that female bounty hunter, ain't you?" she barked, looming over Grace.

She edged back, her mouth dry. This strange woman seemed fairly unhinged.

The preacher cleared his throat. "Excuse me, young lady, perhaps I can help you with something?"

The woman rounded on him, fire in her eyes. "I was talking to her." She stabbed a finger in Grace's direction.

Grace took a deep breath. If she was courageous enough to hunt outlaws, she should be brave enough to face down a hysterical woman. She sat up straighter.

"Yes, I'm a bounty hunter."

The woman took a step back and appraised her from head to toe. "Mighty young, ain't you?"

Grace bristled. "I'm old enough to do what has to be done," she said. Including defending herself against whatever this woman intended to do . . .

As she glared up at her, some of the fight seemed to leak out of the woman's face.

"Sorry. It's just . . . ooh, I could kill —" With a quick glance across the table, she spotted the reverend's collar and stopped abruptly. "You're that preacher fellow?"

Reverend Byington nodded.

"I didn't mean what I said. Truly I didn't. I wouldn't kill no one, but I'm so mad I could spit — well, not spit exactly. Wouldn't be ladylike." She plunked down in a chair. "I'm Clarissa."

Noticing Grace's still-defensive posture, the woman let out a high, almost hysterical cackle. "Y'all thought I was gunning for you? Now, ain't that rich." Clarissa threw back her head and laughed, but it had an angry, nervous edge.

Grace looked over to catch Reverend Byington's eye, but the preacher had his head bent and eyes closed, and he was mumbling to himself.

Clarissa followed her gaze. "Probably praying for a sinner like me," she said with a grimace. "He'd do better to pray you can find that con man who cheated me. Stole my money and took clean off."

Now that she was fairly certain Clarissa's fury and

edginess was directed at someone else, Grace relaxed a bit, though she was still struggling to follow this woman's conversation. Clarissa grabbed her arm, sharp painted claws digging through the thin calico sleeves of Grace's bodice and into her skin. She tried to shake her off but Clarissa held fast, pulling Grace closer until their faces were only inches apart.

"I want you to find that man. You get my money back, I'll give you half. You see that he gets put in jail where he belongs. I'll pay you for that too."

Reverend Byington finally finished praying and looked up with a frown. "I don't think that's wise. Why not inform the sheriff?"

Clarissa shot a withering glance in the preacher's direction, but quickly rearranged her features into a smile that more closely resembled a smirk. "Girls like me, we avoid the law." Then she looked away and muttered under her breath, "Except as paying customers."

Byington's eyes widened. "Perhaps we ought to pray on it before —"

Clarissa threw back her head and laughed again disconcertingly. "You do that, preacher. You do that," she gasped, shaking her head. "Let me ask you, what do you think God —"

Grace interrupted before things went any further. "I'll take the case."

* * *

The next morning, armed with Clarissa's description of the man, his horse, and the direction he'd traveled, Grace saddled Bullet and set off out of Bisbee. Clarissa had insisted on giving her a retainer, assuring Grace that back East, her lawyer father had always requested money before taking a case. And she wanted a contract indicating Grace would give her whatever the con artist had taken. Rather than set the woman off into another rant, Grace accepted the payment and signed. Contract or no, she had always intended to return any money and valuables she recovered, but the retainer was a welcome relief — it would help her survive if the hunt took a while, and she could use some of it to replace her lost lasso.

It turned out the man she was seeking had swindled several gamblers and painted ladies in the area, and Grace knew the town of Rawhide was even more lax about protecting their brothels and saloons, so that's where she planned to head. But as she was about to set Bullet to a canter out of Bisbee, she heard a little voice cry from behind her.

"Grace, wait!"

Eight-year-old Emily Abrams jogged after her and she reined Bullet in, waiting for the little girl to catch up. The young girl often accompanied her mother, who cleaned the rooms over Miz Bessie's saloon, and she'd taken a liking to Grace. When she saw the wanted posters in her room, Emily had been fascinated with her being a bounty hunter, and when Grace collected the same set of flyers of the Guiltless Gang for Emily to study, she and the young girl had become fast friends. But Grace tried not to let herself get too close — whenever she saw the young girl's boundless energy and enthusiasm, the pain of losing her own little sister, Abby, welled up inside her.

Breathless, Emily caught up with Grace but stayed a safe distance from Bullet's stamping hooves. "Ma said you're going bounty hunting. Are you going after the Guiltless Gang? Can I come too?" Emily spoke so rapidly her sentences bumped into each other.

Grace hated to disappoint her, but of course Emily was much too young to help. "I may be on the road for days," she said kindly, humoring the little girl. "Your ma would worry."

"No, she wouldn't. She says you take care of me better than anyone she knows."

"But she'd miss you."

Emily stopped for a moment, a thoughtful look in her eye. "Yes, and I'd miss her too. But Ma says we have to do many things that are hard. I could help, I know I could!"

She sighed — convincing Emily to return home wasn't going to be easy, but Grace really needed to be on her way. She wanted to get to Rawhide and scout out the town before the evening activities began. She dismounted and knelt in front of Emily, laying her hands on the girl's small shoulders and looking her straight in the eye. "Emily, I need you to do a very, very important job for me. Do you think you can do that?"

Eyes shining, Emily stood straighter. "What do I have to do?"

"What I need you to do is go back home. Your ma needs you there to look out for her. Who knows what kind of lowlifes could show up in town tonight?"

Emily looked at her dubiously, sticking her bottom lip out in a pout that reminded Grace achingly of Abby. "You don't want me to help," the girl said.

Her fingers tightened on Emily's shoulders. "I *do* need your help. I'm going to Rawhide to look for a bad man who stole some money. While I'm gone, I also need someone to watch for the Guiltless Gang here in Bisbee. You know exactly what they look like, right? You studied the posters. Can you look out for them for me?"

Emily sniffled a little but nodded. "I'll look at those posters every day. And I'll watch for that gang. Really truly. I promise."

"I know you will. I'm counting on you." She stopped and thought for a moment. "But Emily, if you do see any of them, I need you to wait for me to come back before you do anything. I've been looking for them for a long time, so I need to make sure I catch them myself. All right?"

Emily nodded more emphatically now, and before

Grace could stand, the girl launched herself into Grace's arms and gave her a fierce hug. Grace stiffened, but then slowly, reluctantly, she put her arms around Emily and hugged back. The bittersweet pleasure of hugging her brought up more waves of sadness. Grace would never hug Abby or baby Zeke again.

Her eyes stung and her throat was clogged, and she disengaged herself quickly, turning Emily in the direction of her home.

"I'm counting on you, Emily," she said, clearing her throat and trying to sound bright.

The girl smiled. "When I grow up, I'm going to be the best bounty hunter ever, just like you."

Her chest swelled proudly, Emily hurried back down Main Street to her home and Grace exhaled with relief. "Best bounty hunter ever, huh?" she muttered. She'd have to catch a few more fugitives before she could lay claim to that title . . .

* * *

Hot and dusty, Grace and Bullet finally entered Rawhide. Smaller than Tombstone, the town consisted of only one main road and a few side streets. She rode down each street and alley, noting every saloon and brothel, trying to decide the best place to stalk her quarry. She decided that the stables would be the easiest place to start. The man — Clarissa said he'd called himself Clint, but who knew if that was his real name — had few distinguishing features, so his pure-black horse with a white star on its forehead and white socks might be easier to spot.

Sensing they were approaching another unfamiliar stable, Bullet grew feisty, and Grace reached down to pat his neck. "Come on, boy. You need to behave or no barn here will take you, and we've got a job to do."

She dismounted and tied Bullet outside, peeking inside each stall. In the third one, she found the horse she was looking for. Quickly, she approached the stable hand, an older man with deep creases etched into his forehead that must have come from a perpetual scowl. "Excuse me, sir," she said, trying for a sweet smile. "You don't happen to know where the owner of this horse is staying, do you?"

The man shrugged. Clearly charm wasn't going to work. "I need to find him. It's important."

The man waved a hand toward the stables dismissively. "Can't keep track of all these owners."

Grace pursed her lips in frustration. "Well, I have a horse outside."

"Bring it on in." The man pointed to two vacant stalls. "Take your pick."

Grace handed him her money before she brought Bullet inside, not wanting to give him a chance to change his mind.

Surprisingly, Bullet cooperated — until they reached the stall door. Then he kicked up his usual fuss.

"Hey!" the stable hand called, suddenly more animated now. "Get control of that horse, or he can't stay here."

Grace ignored him, and as she opened the stall door, Bullet went wild, causing the other horses to shriek and neigh in agitation. The man yelled again, but his words were unintelligible over the racket. She managed to get Bullet into the stall, and then stayed outside the door talking to him until he calmed. But as soon as she walked away, her horse squealed and kicked the stall door, making so much noise that he stirred most of the other horses into a frenzy.

"I told you, he can't stay —"

Grace held a hand up, cutting him off. "I've paid, fair and square. Now, if you tell me where the owner of that horse I was asking about went, the sooner I'll be on my way. The longer it takes to find him, the longer my horse stays."

The man scowled and he jerked a finger over his shoulder. "House of ill-repute down the road." Then his eyes widened in horror. "You ain't aiming to spend the whole night with him?"

Grace's face contorted in disgust. "My business with him won't take long."

"Oh, no, you ain't the wronged wife, I hope." His voice turned pleading. "Don't tell him it was me who directed you there. He's a good paying customer here; can't afford to lose him . . ."

She shook her head. "I'm not his wife, and I'm grateful for your help. No need for him to know how I found him."

The stable hand breathed a sigh of relief, and his lips twisted in a ghost of a smile.

Grace headed in the direction the stable hand had pointed, and soon the plink of lively piano music drifted from one of the buildings toward her, along with raucous laughter. She stood outside the doors and steadied her nerves. To catch her prey here, she'd have to use her feminine wiles. To alleviate her disgust, she reminded herself she'd just be play-acting; pretending only long enough to capture a thief — and make her bounty.

She entered and surveyed the room, but several of the men there could have met Clarissa's description. Only one thing she could do. Sashaying up to the bar, she turned enough to keep an eye on most of the men in the room, then forced her voice to an unnaturally loud level but kept it sickeningly sweet.

"I saw the most unusual horse in the stable. It's black with a white star right here." She brushed her finger across her forehead in a circle, then lowered her hand to toy with the button on the high collar of her bodice as if she planned to open it. "I would *love* to meet the owner of that beautiful animal. Maybe he'd take me for a ride."

"I'll take you for a ride, sweetheart," one of the cowboys called out.

"Oh, that sounds delightful," Grace purred, looking

over in the direction of the voice. He could be her mark. "Are you the horse's owner?"

"Uh . . . no, but I'm sure you'd enjoy my horse just as well."

Grace pretended to pout. "I was hoping for *that* horse." She closed her eyes and gave a little shiver, trying to remember how the girls back at Miz Bessie's saloon behaved. "I adore black horses."

The cowboy headed toward her. "Once you see my horse, you'll forget all about that black one."

What could she do now? She had to find some way to discourage him. Grace began to think this might have been a mistake. Clint the con man might not even be here . . . To her right, she noticed an older woman steaming toward her. *Oh, no.*

The woman's graying hair had been pulled up into a cascade of curls on the top of her head, and her low-cut brocade gown covered generous curves that strained the confines of her corset. "This here's my establishment and I'll not have some stranger coming in trying to take work from my girls."

"I-It's not what you think," Grace said in a low voice. "May I talk to you in private?"

The woman eyed her skeptically, but Grace's conservative clothes seemed to convince her. Leading her to a tiny office, she waved toward a seat, but Grace declined. "I'm looking for a man who has a black horse with a star on its forehead. He robbed five people in Bisbee, and he's likely planning to do the same here. I'm a bounty hunter."

The woman's face turned hard and she laughed once mirthlessly. "You had me believing your story there for a minute. Too bad you had to spoil it with that lie at the end."

"I *am* a bounty hunter." But Grace had no way to prove it. "Listen, if you help me find the man, you can take the full payment for his . . . *time* with me. And whether you believe me or not, I'll be saving you and your girls from being swindled."

The woman's expression turned from skeptical to calculating. "You won't expect any pay? Not even if I charge him double?"

Grace shook her head. "Will you help me?"

Without answering, the woman beckoned her to follow. She opened the door and strode back into the saloon room.

"Clint," she called to a man lounging on the couch, dividing his attention between two young women. "One of my girls here admires your horse."

"I heard," he growled. "But I'm busy . . ."

The woman snapped her fingers and both the girls rose and glided from the room.

"Hey!" Clint stared after them longingly, then turned angry eyes to the woman.

"They'll be back." She turned her voice into a coo.

"First, you ought to speak with this young lady. You won't regret it."

Clint stood and headed toward them. The gray-haired woman held out her hand and he slapped some money into her palm.

"You'd better be worth it," he said, frowning as he glanced at Grace's modest outfit. "I don't go for the school-marm look."

She gave him a coy smile. "I'm full of surprises."

"Now, that sounds promising . . ." He came over and took her elbow. "You asked to see my horse? Let's go."

Grace forced herself not to cringe or shrink away as he drew her close. They walked out of the saloon and down the street — it only took a minute, but it was a relief to reach the stables. As he gestured vaguely to his horse and then pressed his body against hers, Grace choked back a gag. Then in one swift move, she slid her hand into his holster, whipped out his gun, and backed away, pointing the revolver at his chest.

"What the devil? What kinda game are you playing, girl?"

Grace lifted an eyebrow. "I hear you're a card cheat. A robber? You like to swindle innocent people out of all their money?"

"*Innocent* people?" He guffawed and gestured toward the brothel. "Can't call any of *those* saloon-dwellers innocent."

"Oh, so I suppose they had it coming?"

Clint didn't respond — instead, he lunged for his gun but Grace stuck out a dainty boot, and he went flying face-first into a nearby pile of manure.

How fitting, she thought. While Clint was still dazed and moaning, she grabbed some rope, tied his arms back good and tight, then hurried into the stable to collect Bullet.

Mounting her horse, she hauled Clint to his feet, tipped her hat to the aghast stable hand, and took off for Bisbee.

CHAPTER 6

As soon as Clarissa had identified Clint, Grace let her search the captive's pockets, from which she extracted several rolls of bills and a leather pouch of gold. The older woman grinned. "This should pay us back for our troubles."

Clint swore at them, but Clarissa only laughed and chucked him under the chin.

"Want a little smooch for old times' sake?" she taunted.

The fury in Clint's eyes as he glared at Clarissa made Grace shiver, and she was relieved to turn him over to the surprised Bisbee sheriff.

After she emerged from the jail, Emily trailed after her, clearly having caught wind of Grace's return.

"You caught that outlaw!" Emily said, bouncing up

and down alongside her as Grace strode down the street. "I've been practicing being a good bounty hunter too. I'm watching for that gang, just like you said. I know all of their faces. I'll tell you as soon as I see any of them!"

Grace smiled at her, though it seemed wishful thinking that any of the gang would turn up on their doorstep. "Thanks, Emily. You're a big help."

Emily beamed. "Are we going to look for them now?"

"Not today. I need some rest."

And she had some debts to clear, now that she had finally made a good bounty, fair and square. *Maybe I can really do this*, she thought hopefully.

* * *

The next morning, Grace galloped off to Tombstone. She'd had a good night's sleep in her room at Miz Bessie's now that her debts were all cleared, but today she was ready to turn her attentions to her own mission. She was heading into the town hoping to finally get more information on the Guiltless Gang.

When she reached the courthouse, several bounty hunters were gathered around the wall of wanted posters.

Deputy Clayton smiled as Grace walked in. "Grace Milton! Heard you caught that Clint Martin before the wanted poster even came out," he said. "Maybe I was wrong about you . . ."

Grace couldn't help feeling pleased at his admission,

but a few of the other bounty hunters turned to her and sniggered. "Pretty stupid criminal to get himself caught by a woman," one murmured.

"So where's the latest posters, deputy?" called another.

The deputy held up two flyers. "This one here's for Clint, but Miss Milton there already took care of it." He tossed that poster onto his desk, then pushed back his chair and tacked the other poster to the wall.

"Couldn't even get a handful of feed for my horse with that reward," the tallest man complained. "What's he wanted for?"

The man next to him ran a finger over the words at the bottom of the poster. "Just torturing and killing some Injuns." He directed a condemning sneer at the quiver of arrows Grace had slung over her shoulder. "He's no outlaw. *He* should be getting a reward for that. You won't catch me turning in such a man."

A chorus of "me neither" followed.

Grace frowned, her blood blazing through her veins. "Let me see that flyer. I'll go after him myself."

"Ha! You do that, girlie. You got lucky once, but Injun killers are a lot more dangerous than gentleman gamblers," one of the men scoffed.

Grace elbowed her way past the group to look at the poster. It sickened her to read what this man had done. She was glad it seemed none of the people he'd tortured had been Ndeh, but he deserved to be strung up, not left to roam free. She stared at the poster, memorizing the man's every feature. She didn't care how small the reward, she'd do it even if she received no payment at all.

"Last seen heading toward the Dragoon Mountains," the man who'd taunted her read. He shook his head. "I don't know, girl. That's pretty dangerous territory. Renegade Apache hide out in those hills. Even the U.S. Army ain't been able to capture all of them."

"They're not *Apache*. They're Ndeh," Grace said through clenched teeth.

"Oh, look out, boys." The heavy man beside Grace sniggered and backed away from her mockingly. "We got ourselves an Injun-lover here. No telling what she done with those savages."

Grace squeezed her eyes shut and balled her fists to control her temper. No way would she give these men the satisfaction of seeing how much their teasing upset her. Reining in her fury, she turned and tipped her head to Deputy Clayton.

"Good day, deputy. I'll be back with your man."

Head high, Grace stalked from the sheriff's office and out of the courthouse.

* * *

Two days later, Grace led the bound criminal down the streets of Tombstone. She had tracked the man through the mountains, where she'd found him weak, having run out of food and water. She'd felt no sympathy for him. Now he was trussed to his horse, throwing insults at Grace as crowds jeered.

"This here's an Injun-lover," he called to the gathering people. "A-all I done is take care of some of those low-down varmints so as they didn't scalp our women and children."

Some in the crowd began to heckle her, and she edged closer to her prisoner. "Want me to tell them how brave you really are?" she hissed. "I could tell how you crawled on the ground begging for mercy when I lassoed you."

The man winced. "You say that, and I'll come gunning for you when I get out."

"You do that." Grace looked him in the eye, but he glanced away. "Who'd win in a fast draw?"

The man spent the rest of the journey to the jail in silence, head down. The crowd dispersed once Grace led him into the courthouse.

As soon as Deputy Clayton had locked the man into a cell, he returned to his office. "Good work, Grace," he said, handing her the reward money. "I'm not afraid to admit, it seems you really are getting the hang of this." His look held genuine surprise and admiration.

She turned to the wall of wanted posters and noticed no new bounties hung on the wall. She returned to studying the faces of the Guiltless Gang, despite having long ago imprinted every detail of them in her memory — before she'd even had an inkling about becoming a bounty hunter. Their faces had been burned there since they took her family from her. "What about these outlaws?" She gestured toward the gang. "Any news on their whereabouts?"

Deputy Clayton shook his head. "Now, Grace. Those Guiltless are too dangerous for you to handle. You've done some impressive work catching petty criminals," he emphasized the word *petty*, "and you got lucky with Doc Slaughter."

Lucky? Luck had nothing to do with it. Her skill and speed had saved her life and that of the girl Slaughter was attacking. Blood pounded so hard in Grace's ears that she barely heard the deputy continue.

"It's not a job for a girl. Let the experienced bounty hunters do their jobs, and stick to the small rewards like you been doing. That way you won't offend the men."

"*Offend the men?*" Grace said incredulously. "What, because I'm a faster draw and a better shot? If that offends them, then maybe they should practice until they can beat me."

The deputy frowned. "Now, don't get too big for your britches is my advice. Ain't becoming in a lady. No man wants to marry a woman who's a better shot and lets him know it."

Grace was about to retort when she had a sudden thought. Deputy Clayton was wrong; she knew one man who might just admit that, and want her still. Joe. And he was the one who'd taught her those skills, or at least honed what her father had started. Pangs of guilt and sadness shot into her heart from different directions, and Joe still filled her thoughts as she walked from the courthouse and mounted Bullet. Deputy Clayton's jibes made her even more determined to track the Guiltless Gang down. She had enough money to live on for now; all she needed was one clue to get started.

Every step she made toward finding them might also be one closer to a time she could consider being with Joe.

CHAPTER 7

Grace stayed late in Tombstone, questioning everyone she could about the Guiltless Gang. They all claimed to have heard nothing, but she wondered if they were telling her the truth. The deputy was more than likely right — people did not like the idea of a girl trying to hunt down such a gang.

By the time she returned to Bisbee, only a few men sat slumped over their drinks, but she thought she may as well try asking around there as well.

"They're all full as a tick," the bartender said as he noticed her attempts. "Not worth questioning. Best to ask 'em earlier in the evening when they're just starting to get roostered up."

She tried a little longer, but the barman was right — she got no more information than she had in Tombstone. Dejected, she climbed the stairs to her room and, remembering the drunkard, wedged a chair under the doorknob after she locked the door.

Once again, nightmares about the burning cabin and of the gang's faces kept her tossing and turning all night.

When she went downstairs the next morning, the saloon was abuzz. As Grace passed one of the painted ladies, frowning curiously at the fuss, she asked what was going on.

"You didn't hear what happened to Caroline Abrams?"

Emily's mother? Normally Grace ignored gossip but this she had to hear. Her heart quickened as she asked. "What's happened?" She braced herself for the worst.

The woman lowered her voice. "A dapper gentleman came calling on her last night, pretending to be lost, but then he shoved his way into Caroline's cabin and tried to force himself on her."

Grace went white. "Is she all right? And what about Emily?"

"I think they're both all right; must have been a lucky escape. Caroline sent word she wouldn't be in to work today, though. All I know is they call the man 'Black Coat' on account of his dapper clothes. Looks like a fine gentleman in his black frock coat and gray silk vest with some swirly design on it. Tries to romance the ladies first, then steals from them. Hilda says he done preyed on other widows out Tombstone's way."

"I'd better check on Caroline and Emily," Grace said, rushing outside, where she almost bumped into Deputy Clayton.

"Whoa there." Clayton grasped her arm to steady her. "Grace! Where are you rushing? Off to chase another outlaw?" He chuckled.

"Deputy, I'm glad you're here. You investigating this Black Coat attack? I hear he's been causing trouble round Tombstone too."

"Who? Oh, the man bothering the widows?" Deputy Clayton shook his head. "No, no. I'm here for the sheriff's help. My posse is all working the bank robbery in the next county. We're drafting sheriff's departments from around the area to help locate the perpetrators."

Grace looked at him, shocked. "But surely you have someone working the Black Coat case? He's attacking vulnerable women."

Clayton sighed apologetically. "I just don't have anyone available right now. The only men not on this bank case are the best bounty hunters in the state — the Watkins brothers."

She almost choked. The most *notorious* bounty hunters in the state was more like it.

"Thing is, I need the Watkinses to guard and transport a fugitive across state lines to Nevada."

"So no one's looking for Black Coat?"

The deputy's cheeks reddened. "I do what I can to try and keep the local women safe, but it'd be best for widows to come into town and not be out on their own. Can't imagine why any woman would put herself at risk like that. Why don't you spread the word a little, if you can?"

She couldn't believe what she was hearing. "The sheriff here in Bisbee won't be looking into it either?"

"I told you." The deputy's voice sharpened with impatience. "We're all needed to catch those bank robbers. Like I say, maybe you could warn the women to stay in town until Black Coat is apprehended."

With that, he tipped his hat and rushed toward the sheriff's office.

Grace stared after him. She would saddle up Bullet and check on Emily and Caroline herself, and see that they moved into town. But she had no idea which other women lived alone in the hills outside Bisbee. How could she possibly find and warn them?

"Grace?" Reverend Byington hurried up to her. "I'm so glad I found you. I've been counseling Caroline Abrams and her young daughter. Caroline is so distraught she can hardly speak, and Emily insists that they both need to see you."

She nodded quickly. "I was just heading out to their homestead."

The preacher gestured toward a nearby boarding house.

"I've convinced them to stay here for a few days. It's not safe in the hills with that outlaw running loose."

"And the lawmen not chasing him," Grace muttered.

Reverend Byington raised a questioning eyebrow.

"Deputy Clayton insists they have a more important case — a bank robbery." Her tone was so sarcastic that the preacher glanced at her in surprise. "And according to him, the best bounty hunters in the state" — Grace choked on the words — "the Watkins brothers, are transporting a fugitive across state lines. So everyone's too busy."

"That's unfortunate," the preacher murmured, and the sympathy in his eyes indicated that he wasn't only referring to the lack of law enforcement.

"It's more than unfortunate," Grace burst out. "It's *criminal* that women and children aren't important enough to protect."

"Now, now, my dear. I'm sure they care about the victims. They're already overworked —"

"All Deputy Clayton offered as a solution was to tell the women who live alone to come into town."

"Well, that's an excellent idea. In fact, I'll take up a collection to pay their expenses, and then go out to warn them. I think I know where most of the vulnerable families are in the area."

Grace shook her head. "But that doesn't solve the problem. What about this Black Coat? He might get away while the lawmen are *busy*."

"I'll make it a matter of prayer."

She wanted to shout that prayer didn't help. Hadn't she prayed that her parents would survive? If prayer worked, why did so many bad things keep happening? Had Caroline prayed for safety?

"For now," the preacher continued, "would you come with me to see Caroline and her daughter?"

"Of course."

Grace accompanied Reverend Byington to the boarding house, where Caroline sat huddled on a sofa in the parlor, sobbing.

Emily sat beside her mother, patting her shoulder, but when they entered, the little girl jumped up and hurried toward them.

"Grace!" She grabbed her hand and tugged her toward the sofa. "Ma, Grace is here. She'll help us."

The preacher slowly lowered himself into a nearby chair, but Grace just stood awkwardly as Caroline lifted her head, swabbed at her watery eyes with a handkerchief, and eyed Grace for a moment. Then in a tear-choked voice, she said, "My daughter is convinced you can help us. I'm sorry she dragged you over here. There's nothing you can do."

Rather than contradict her, Grace asked gently, "What happened, Mrs. Abrams?"

Caroline shook her head and buried her face in her handkerchief.

Emily pulled Grace to the other end of the sofa. "I'll tell you," she said quietly. "Ma's too upset."

Grace sat down and looked at Emily encouragingly as she began.

"We were finishing dinner when this man knocked on the door. Ma didn't want to answer but, he called out that he was lost. She told me to go up into the attic."

"And did you?" Knowing how inquisitive Emily was, Grace doubted that she'd obeyed.

The girl glanced at her mother. "I went . . . but I peeked downstairs. Ma opened the door only a little ways, but the man shoved it open the whole way and grabbed her arms. Then he pushed her onto the floor."

Caroline sobbed a little louder, and Emily turned to her. "I didn't let him hurt you, did I, Ma?" She turned back to Grace. "I grabbed the fire poker and whacked him on the back and head. He howled and let go of her —"

Caroline interrupted. "Emily," she said, her voice shaking, "you know you shouldn't have done something so dangerous."

"But I saved you."

Her mother sniffed again but pulled her daughter close to her. "He could have shot you. Shot us both," she scolded, though her voice was filled with love.

"But he didn't. I kept hitting him. He tried to grab me, but I kept jumping out of his way." She turned to Grace again. "That's what bounty hunters do, isn't it?"

"Well . . ." She certainly didn't want to encourage the little girl to be rash. "Bounty hunters must be very, very careful, Emily. Your mother's right, it could have been really dangerous."

She looked miffed. "I was careful. I was careful not to get caught. Right, Ma?"

"Oh, Emily . . ." Caroline shook her head.

The girl thrust out her lower lip. "I was being brave. Wasn't I, Grace?"

"I'm sure you were, but your ma is worried that you could have been hurt. And she wouldn't want to lose you."

Emily's eyes took on a faraway look. "Like my pa?"

Grace sent a questioning look toward the preacher.

He looked somber. "I buried William Abrams a few months ago."

She rested a hand on the little girl's knee. "Yes, like your pa," she said softly. "No wonder your ma is so upset."

"That thief stole my husband's pocket watch and all the horses," Caroline told Grace, more tears threatening. "The only things I had left of William." She twisted her damp handkerchief into knots between her fingers.

"I'm so sorry." She knew what it was like to lose every tangible connection to your loved ones. The anguish of thinking she had lost the only picture of her family was still fresh in her mind.

If it hadn't been for Reverend Byington finding it in the desert, it would have been gone forever.

Emily broke into Grace's thoughts. "You can find that man, can't you, Grace? You'll get back the horses and Pa's watch. You're the best bounty hunter in the whole state. Right?" She looked to Reverend Byington for confirmation.

"Grace has certainly captured quite a few outlaws in a few short months," he said, though his face held worry.

"You have?" Caroline's strangled voice held a note of disbelief.

"I told you that, Ma." Emily leaned close to Grace and confided, "I can tell you what he looks like. I've been practicing by memorizing those wanted posters."

Grace looked at her keenly. Could this little girl really have a good description?

"Go on."

"Well, he had bushy eyebrows that almost met in the middle, and a moustache like this." Emily drew a finger under her nose and curved it down. "And his nose was crooked right here." She pointed to the bridge of her own nose. "Oh, and he had a white scar." She traced a short line across her chin.

"That's excellent," Grace told her. "You really are observant."

Reverend Byington rose. "I need to warn other widows in the area who are living alone to come into town until the man is caught," he said quietly, then turned toward Caroline. "I hope you'll be comfortable here."

"Oh, preacher, I can't be beholden to you like this. I want to pay my own bill but . . ." Her tears started again. "All our money was tied up in those horses. I planned to sell them so Emily and I could go back East to live with my family . . ."

Grace's heart ached for Caroline. She also knew how it felt to lose everything and to be beholden to the preacher. As much as she wanted to find the Guiltless Gang, she had to help Emily and her mother first. And she had an idea of how to do that.

Grace stood as Byington went to the door. He eyed her suspiciously.

"Could I accompany you to warn the widows?" she asked innocently.

The preacher's gaze pinned her. The concern in his eyes made her squirm, but she knew she couldn't let that criminal hurt anyone else.

She'd find Black Coat, and when she did, she'd also be able to help Caroline get to the East Coast where she and Emily would be safer. Once there, the little girl would soon forget all about bounty hunting.

Grace just had to put her idea into action first — and she couldn't have the preacher trying to stop her. He'd never agree to her plan for luring the criminal into a honey trap.

But she'd need an empty cabin for her plan to work . . .

CHAPTER 8

By the time she and Reverend Byington returned to town with the vulnerable women from the surrounding areas, Grace had already selected the perfect cabin in which to put her plan into action. She bid farewell to the preacher and the women, then made her way to the general store for supplies — but as she walked through the door, she collided into someone. Someone tall, tanned, and muscular, with beautiful dark eyes and a broad-brimmed hat that contrasted with his buckskin clothing . . .

"Joe?"

He grasped her arm to prevent her from falling, and Grace's breath caught in her throat. Being so close to him, feeling the warmth of his touch, brought back a rush of memories that set every nerve tingling. But as soon as he realized it was her, Joe's eyes widened and he flinched. He yanked back his hand as if he'd been bitten by a snake. Then he brushed past her without a word.

So he did hate her? Grace felt as if her insides were shriveling.

She turned and stared after him. What was he doing in Bisbee?

"Joe, wait," she called. He stopped but didn't face her.

"What?" His voice had a rough, harsh edge.

"C-can we talk?"

"About what?"

His clipped tone made it clear he had no interest in speaking to her and that the burning questions in her heart were better left unsaid. Still, she couldn't let him walk off without at least *trying* to explain. She marched down the sidewalk determinedly, her boots clunking on the wooden planks, and stepped in front of Joe, forcing him to look at her. But once she'd reached him, her bravado waned once again. "Uh . . . wh-what brings you to Bisbee?"

"Getting supplies."

The stiffness of his mouth and the way Joe avoided her eyes only made Grace ache for him more. "Oh? Reverend Byington said you bought supplies for the Ndeh last week. They ran out already?"

Joe's cheeks flushed and he shifted from side to side. "Um, no. Not exactly."

What did that mean?

"It's just that . . . well, I needed supplies for myself," he said, shuffling his moccasins on the wooden sidewalk.

Grace felt her eyebrows draw together in confusion. He couldn't buy those supplies in Tombstone? Joe shouldered his heavy pack and stared off into the distance. His face was almost as crimson as the bandana around his neck.

"I needed some time alone, so I planned to go camping," he continued, risking a glance at her. His expression seemed to run through a whole range of emotions, and Grace's heartbeat doubled. "I should be going —"

She placed a hand on his arm. "Joe, please . . . don't go. Can't we talk, just for a moment?"

"Nothing to talk about."

The hurt that lay behind his words cut her to ribbons. She hadn't meant to hurt him, but how could she convince him of that?

"Couldn't we just go into the saloon and get a drink? Then you can be on your way."

"Right now?"

Was it her imagination, or did he sound hopeful?

"Yes. I can come back later to buy my supplies."

Joe shrugged, clearly working to seem indifferent.

When they were settled at a table with a bottle of sarsaparilla, Grace reached across the table and tentatively set her hand on his. He stared down at it like he couldn't believe it was there, but he didn't move his hand away.

"Joe, I'm sorry," she began. "I didn't mean to hurt you. Truly I didn't." How could she explain why she left when she wasn't completely sure herself? Now that he was there, in front of her, it seemed like madness to consider not being with him. She took a deep breath, trying to gain control of her emotions.

He swallowed hard. "It's all right." His voice was husky, so husky that Grace knew he didn't mean what he'd said.

"The last thing I wanted to do was leave you, but —"

"Then why did you?"

"You know why," she said. She didn't know how to say it, so she put it as simply as she could. "I have to find the Guiltless Gang."

Joe stared straight into her eyes. "It's not your job to bring them in, Grace. You need to just . . ." He tailed off, letting out a short burst of air exasperatedly. "You have to let go of this desire for revenge."

She didn't break his stare, but she shook her head. "I won't rest until every last one of those murderers is behind bars . . . I *can't*," she said quietly.

Joe pulled his hand from hers and poured their drinks, then thumped the bottle down on the table. "Even though I disagreed with what you were doing, I understood how you felt. I still do. That's why I offered to accompany you. But then when I woke up and found you *gone* . . . ?" He pursed his lips and stared off into space, shaking his own head now.

Grace ran a finger around the rim of her glass. The condensation wet her fingertips and she rubbed the moisture on her heated cheeks. "I-I got scared —"

"Scared?" Joe whispered. "Of what? I'd never hurt you."

"Not of being hurt." Grace hesitated. She didn't want to tell him the full reason why she'd left, but it wasn't fair to let him think it was his fault. She stared down at the table and took a deep breath. "I was scared of what I felt for you. Too scared to stay. Too scared to have you travel with me. I . . . I was worried my feelings for you would stop me from my mission."

She glanced up and Joe stared back at her, his eyes softening at her confession. "But I already told you I wouldn't," he said in a low voice. "I wanted to go with you. To protect you."

Grace felt her shoulders slump. That was part of the problem; love and revenge didn't mix. She wanted — needed — to take care of herself and handle her own problems.

"Joe, I was afraid I'd go soft. Too soft to track criminals, to do what needs to be done without worrying that my actions might hurt you. If it wasn't for all this, I would never have left. But I did it because I thought I'd lose my drive for revenge." She paused for a moment, embarrassment sending hot prickles up the back of her neck. "Whenever I'm around you, I become a different person. Softer, more . . . gentle."

"Nothing wrong with that." For the first time since she'd bumped into him, Joe's lips curved into a slight smile. "Same thing happens to me."

"It does?" The tenderness in his eyes made Grace melt inside like the puddle of water under her glass. Abruptly, she broke their gaze. This was exactly what she'd been afraid of.

"I can't do this . . ."

"Do what?"

"Let you distract me."

"I'm distracting you?" Joe said, his eyes sparkling a little now, playfully.

She stamped a dainty boot under the table. "Stop looking at me that way."

Joe hesitated for a moment, then reached over and stroked the back of her hand softly. "Does this distract you too?" His voice was low, velvety.

The fluttering in her chest made it impossible for Grace to speak. Part of her wanted to tear her hand away, but the part that won wanted to stay that way forever and never leave this spot.

"You haven't answered me."

Joe laid his palm flat on her hand now, but she shook it off.

"Don't," she said softly. "You're already confusing me enough."

Joe laughed. "What's so confusing?"

Grace relished the sound of his laugh for a moment, but now that she'd told him what she had needed to, she couldn't let it change things. She leaned back in her chair. "I need to think straight."

Joe leaned closer and held out his hands, a pleading look in his eyes. "But we could do this, Grace. Together."

She could barely get out the words. "No, Joe. I . . . I've told you —"

He gave her a rueful look. "I know. I'm too much of a distraction."

Grace smiled at his sulky expression. "Yes. And I can't afford any. Not right now, anyway."

Suddenly, Joe's whole body went rigid. "You've tracked down one of the gang, haven't you?"

"No." She couldn't keep the disappointment from her voice. "No one knows their whereabouts."

Joe visibly relaxed again.

"But for now," she continued, "I have a bounty case I need to pursue, and after that I do intend to track down the Guiltless."

"Oh, Grace, I hoped you'd rethink that. Bounty hunting?"

She felt her jaw clench. "Not you too, Joe. It's how I make my living now. People just have to accept it, you included."

He sighed and nodded slowly. "Well, I hope it's just another petty criminal. I . . . I heard about the recent arrest you made. Seems like you've made a few enemies in this town."

Grace smiled a little. "You've been checking up on me, haven't you? That's why you're in town?"

Joe flushed red again but he didn't deny it.

"Well, this man I'm seeking's been preying on vulnerable widows on the outskirts of town — attacking them, then stealing their money and goods."

"Sounds dangerous," Joe began with a frown, but she raised an eyebrow and he stopped and sighed. "So you know where this criminal is? I could go with you . . . maybe help out?"

"Joe . . ." Didn't he hear what she'd just told him? But the aching thought of leaving him again was making her consider backing down from her decision to do things alone. He wasn't going to like her idea for trapping Black Coat, though.

"What?" Joe studied her.

"I have a plan," Grace whispered. Even if she couldn't explain everything here, the saloon was a good place to get rumors started. "Play along with me, please?" Grace kept her voice so low Joe had to lean across the table to hear. He took a deep breath as he moved closer to her, and again she had to work to steady her own emotions. "I'll explain later," she said quickly.

When Joe nodded, Grace sat up straighter in her chair.

"Actually, I'm going to take a break from bounty

hunting for a little while." She spoke loudly enough so that everyone around her could hear.

"Oh?" His eyebrows pulled together a little, but he went along with her.

"You know how I helped my pa break horses?" It ached a little to mention it, but Joe nodded, his eyes brimming with curiosity.

"Well, I promised Widow Burns I'd take care of her horses while she's staying here in town."

As she'd expected, one of the saloon girls was watching and listening, and as soon as Grace finished speaking, the girl turned and whispered to her friend. Joe looked at the group, then turned back and raised an eyebrow.

"Are you sure that's a good idea —"

"I'll be fine," Grace interjected, not having to pretend much now. She'd said similar things so many times. "I'm not sure why everyone is so worried about staying out in the hills alone. Besides, a promise is a promise." She smiled nonchalantly, drained her glass, and then stood up and headed for the door, Joe close on her heels. She could hear more whispers beginning around her — her ploy seemed to have worked.

As soon as they got outside, Joe steered her into a deserted alley. "That was play-acting, right? You aren't seriously planning to —" He broke off when she flashed him an annoyed look. "So you do intend to go after him," he said flatly.

"No, not go after him. I'm going to lure him to me. The Burns horses are stabled at an isolated homestead, and I know the thief stole horses last night, so I expect he'll be interested in these ones when he knows the owner is gone." He'd also be interested in a woman staying alone.

"Grace, you can't take on this man alone. I'm coming with you."

"You can't." She paused. "If he knows I have a man around, he won't show up."

Joe stared at her as the realization of what she meant sank in. He shook his head. "I can't leave you unprotected, not with someone like that lurking around."

"You have to —"

"I'll camp somewhere nearby," Joe interjected, his jaw hardened. "I . . . I can't bear the thought of letting you stay out there on your own."

Grace considered it — if he was a safe distance away, it might be okay. He leaned closer, sensing her dubiousness.

"Who taught you to sneak up on someone so silently they'd never hear you coming?" he said in a low voice. "Who taught you how to blend in with the trees and rocks so you could move through the forest undetected?"

She took a breath. "You."

"Exactly. No one will know I'm there. No one but you."

Grace relented. "Fine. But we need to be sure everyone sees us leave separately."

"Of course." Joe grinned. "I'll wait until dusk and ride

out of town in a different direction. No one will suspect a thing."

She looked up at him, feeling an overwhelming sense of gratitude. After everything that had happened, and as frustrating as it was, he still cared enough to want to look out for her.

When Grace took off on Bullet, Joe remained behind, watching her go.

*   *   *

A few hours later, she had reached the cabin, fed the horses, and fixed some hominy for her dinner. She felt for the steeds — if she hadn't planned this ruse, they most likely would have been left alone for a few days while Widow Burns was in town. The widow seemed to have taken most of her possessions with her, leaving the cabin bare of decorations and making it look almost unlived in. Grace made the austere room homier by propping the tintype of her family on the mantelpiece. She couldn't help thinking about sharing a cabin like this with Joe . . .

What would it be like to have Joe around all the time, for them not to be worrying about stopping criminals? Just being together . . . ? Grace forced such thoughts away. Like she'd told him, notions like that were too dangerous, too distracting.

Instead, she concentrated on cleaning and loading her gun. Then she selected the best vantage points for keeping a lookout in the cabin. Once it grew dark, she'd leave a candle burning on the mantelpiece but hide out here near the door. If Black Coat was lurking and keeping watch, he wouldn't see her standing in the shadows beside the window. She only hoped he *would* turn up, and that it would be soon.

As Grace rechecked the door to be sure it was securely locked, a distant sound startled her. She froze with her hand on the latch. A horse, thundering up the trail to the cabin. Grace's heart pounded faster than the cantering hoofbeats. As far as she knew, Joe wouldn't arrive until dusk, and in any case, he shouldn't be coming anywhere near the cabin — they'd agreed. Was it Black Coat already?

Steeling herself, she leaned in closer to the door and waited.

CHAPTER 9

"Grace?" a voice shouted outside the door.

It *was* Joe! What was he doing here? The nerves coursing through her body switched to anger, and she yanked the door open and marched out onto the porch. "You promised me you'd keep your distance! Black Coat won't show up with you here, I told you that."

Joe was still mounted on his horse, Paint, who he nosed toward the porch. He pointed behind him. "Dust storm's coming," he retorted. "I wanted to be sure you were safe."

Grace looked in the direction he was pointing. A swirling cloud of white was approaching Bisbee in the distance, but it was far enough away that they were all right for the time being.

"Looks like a thunderstorm's chasing its tail," Joe added as Grace put her hands on her hips. When she looked more closely, she realized he was right. Further in the distance, ominous gray clouds hung low in the sky, but that didn't tamp down her annoyance. Her worries that Joe would interfere with her bounty hunting were proving true.

"Don't look at me like that," he said when he saw her frown. "Your outlaw most likely hasn't even got word about you being isolated out here yet. Chances are he won't drift into the saloon until this evening, and with the dust storm I doubt he'll head up out here tonight."

Grace sighed. "You're probably right."

Joe turned and followed her gaze down toward the swirling cloud below them. "We're probably safe from the worst of it here in any case. Most dust storms peter out when they hit the hills."

Grace bit back the question nagging in her brain. If he was so sure the storm would weaken, then why had he come to the cabin? She watched him closely and pulled the door wider. "May as well come in now that you're here," she said grudgingly.

Joe dismounted and shouldered his pack. "No, I just wanted to check on you, to let you know the storm was coming. Like I said, it shouldn't hit here too bad. I'll just set up camp like I planned."

She frowned a little. "All right. Well, why don't you put Paint in the paddock with Bullet?" Her horse would be glad for company. He disliked most, but he'd befriended Paint and the other Ndeh horses. With Bullet's dread of stalls, Grace hadn't stabled him with Widow Burns's other horses. Instead she released him into the paddock so he could run free. When Joe led Paint to the gate, Bullet raced toward them, mane flying, and he and Paint nosed each other. They both whickered as if greeting an old friend, and she couldn't help wondering if Bullet missed life with the Ndeh as much as she did.

As soon as the horses were secured, Joe followed Grace back to the porch, hesitating when she opened the door. He peered inside, and his gaze lit on the tintype propped on the mantelpiece. "Making the place home-like, huh?" he said lightly.

Grace swallowed. No place could ever be like home again.

Sensing her silence, Joe turned to her, his face tight with remorse. "Oh, Grace, I'm so sorry. I didn't mean to —"

"It's all right," she whispered, but she had trouble pushing words past the lump in her throat.

"No, it's not. I should have thought before I spoke," he said in a soft voice. "I know what it's like."

The gentleness of his words made tears well in Grace's eyes. She couldn't speak, only nod. He'd lost his parents too, and the Ndeh had adopted him when he was eight. She wondered if anyone ever got over their whole world falling apart.

Joe cleared his throat. "Are you sure you'll be all right this evening?"

Grace kept her voice as even as she could. "I'll be fine. I'm a bounty hunter, remember?" The declaration came out more clipped than she'd intended.

"Right. How could I forget?"

Hurt colored Joe's voice, and Grace immediately felt bad.

"Have you eaten?" she ventured. "I could make you something —"

"Thanks for the offer, but I brought my own food." He threw his pack over his shoulder again. "Now that I know you're all right, I'll find a place to camp for the night." He started to turn, his back as stiff as his words.

"Wait," Grace pleaded.

Joe stopped but kept his gaze on the ground in front of him. "Maybe . . . maybe I should stay close by tonight," he muttered. "You might need help if the storm does end up heading this way. If it's all right with you, I'll shelter in the barn."

"Why don't you sleep inside the cabin? It'll be safer." *From the storm, at least.* "Like you say, this criminal isn't likely to roam the hills in a storm."

"The barn will be just fine." Joe's gruffness seemed to be masking something, and when he glanced over his shoulder at her, she saw dejection, concern . . . and passion burning in his eyes.

"Don't go yet, please?" she whispered.

He shook his head as if dislodging thoughts that plagued him. "This'll be better for both of us."

"All right," she said resignedly. She tried to breathe away her longing to reach out for him. Her own heart, too tender, too confused, wouldn't withstand another rejection.

"Good night, Grace."

Though his voice was tender, Joe's words sounded so final, so distant. Would she see him again in the morning?

* * *

A flash of lightning and a clap of thunder startled Grace awake. Outside, wind howled like a wild beast and beat against the wooden walls of the unfamiliar cabin. Dust whistled through chinks in the planks, scraping her skin and covering every surface with grit. At first she thought it was another nightmare — that she was once again struggling through the flying embers in her family's home, her baby brother cradled limply in her arms. But then she remembered where she was, and she stumbled to the wooden ladder leading down from the loft. Her chemise hem bunched in one hand, she backed down into the darkness below, one shaky step at a time, listening to the window rattling as sand scratched across it. She was worried it would crack.

She rushed over, unlatched the door, and tried to inch it open, but gusts snatched the handle from her hands, banging it back and forth. Grace jumped out of the way as the door blew wide open suddenly and slammed against the wall, allowing swathes of sand to sweep across the room.

"Joe!" she called into the dust-filled night, but there was no answer. Again and again, she shrieked his name, but the wind tore the words from her mouth and drowned out her frantic cries. Leaning against the door with all her strength, she pushed and shoved until finally she managed to fight it closed. The wind thumped against it in a steady rhythm, but she realized she couldn't just stay inside.

Bullet. She needed to get him into the barn with the other horses, and Paint too. Wondering if Joe had woken yet — she couldn't imagine how he could sleep through this — she grabbed a tea towel and dipped it into the standing dishwater, then wrapped it over her nose and mouth to protect against the flying dust. Then, draping a shawl over her head and tucking it around her for extra protection, she wrestled the door open. Shielding her eyes with her arms, Grace hurried out toward the paddock.

Joe was already there — she could see him up ahead, a bandana wound around his face. He clutched at Paint's lead, but was struggling to calm Bullet, who was screaming and rearing in the commotion.

"Joe! Leave him! Take Paint to the barn!" Grace shouted over to him, but her words, muffled by the towel, were drowned out by the fury of the storm.

Bits of sand pelted and stung her skin as she raced across the field toward them and tapped Joe on the shoulder. He jumped and whirled around, but seeing her, he visibly relaxed.

Grace motioned to the barn, and Joe nodded and rushed toward it with Paint. She lifted the towel to call for Bullet, and bits of sand and dirt smacked her in the face, grit filling her mouth, gagging her. She bent against the wind and spit out what she could, dropping the towel back into place and chasing after Bullet. The horse kicked and thrashed so much she couldn't get close to him, and his shrieks only added to the eeriness and noise of the storm. Lightning flashed again, followed by an ear-splitting boom. Bullet tore across the field, and Joe ran back out to her, trying to get her to come inside, but Grace ignored him. She knew Bullet would settle if she could just get the horse's attention. Hunched against the wind, Grace raced toward him, but before she reached him, the whirling dust thinned. Without warning, lightning zigzagged across the sky and thunder exploded nearby. Rain gushed suddenly from the heavens, soaking Grace to the skin and dampening the grit from the dust into sandy puddles. The gray clouds must have reached overhead now, chasing away the sandstorm . . .

She pulled the towel away from her mouth and yelled for Bullet, her voice hoarse. The horse stopped mid-buck and his hooves crashed to the ground. He looked at Grace and then trotted obediently toward her, finally, just as Joe ran up to her, his hat sending rivulets of water cascading around him. He handed her Bullet's lead and halter, but Grace struggled to get it on in the blinding rain, her waterlogged shawl hampering her movements. Yanking the shawl off in frustration, she tossed it over one shoulder, and Bullet eventually allowed her to put on his halter and lead him to the barn and into a stall. He remained calm while she rubbed him down, but as soon as she walked out and shut the stall door, he grew wild again.

"Hush now," she begged. "You can't stay outside in this storm."

As if to prove her point, thunder crashed overhead.

"He'll settle eventually," Joe called from the doorway. "*You* need to get dry, before you catch a chill."

With one last plea to Bullet, Grace turned and went over to Joe. Crouching low, they raced across the open field, and she stopped briefly at the pump to rinse her gritty teeth. Before she could prime it, Joe nudged her and pointed up to the deluge falling down on them, and they both laughed. Tilting her head to the sky, she took in mouthfuls of water, rinsing her mouth, and beside her Joe did the same. She felt her braid unravel, and her sopping hair dripped over her face. She brushed it back from her forehead and turned toward Joe. He stared at her as if mesmerized. Pinned by his gaze, Grace paused, one hand to her hair. The heat in his stare seared her. Drowning in the depths of his eyes, she slowly lowered her hand and her fingers brushed the dripping fringe of her shawl. The flames Joe had lit in her body spread to her cheeks. She'd forgotten to put the shawl back on and she realized that her wet chemise clung to every curve.

Cheeks burning, Grace fumbled for the shawl, dragging it around her and trying to hold the wet fabric out and away from her body.

Unable to look at Joe, she turned and rushed up the porch steps.

CHAPTER 10

"You'd better come in and dry off," Grace muttered over her shoulder, embarrassment making her words stiff and unwelcoming.

"I'm better off out here," Joe said, his own voice a little hoarse.

She turned and looked down at him with a sigh. "Joe, don't be ridiculous. You're soaked, and the storm is still fierce."

Joe looked at her a moment longer, and then clumped up onto the porch. "I won't stay long, maybe just help you get a fire going."

"I can . . ." Grace wanted to say she could do it herself, but she wouldn't be able to keep her shawl wrapped around her like this and carry logs. Besides, she realized she shouldn't be so hard on him — he was only trying to help.

They went inside and Joe headed for the log pile beside the fireplace. He muttered something under his breath, and then said, "I . . . I should take off my shirt; I'm dripping everywhere. I better wring it out so it can start to dry."

Grace stared as he pulled the buckskin shirt over his head. She'd seen Joe without a shirt before, but he'd been covered in war paint or bear grease. And it hadn't been so noticeable in the Indian camp where children ran around naked. But here, alone in the cabin, watching his muscles ripple as he wrung the shirt into the sink and lay it flat near the fire, then as he picked up logs and stacked them in the fireplace — it did dangerous things to her insides. She knew she should turn away, but she couldn't.

Joe turned and surprised her, catching her staring. Grace's face burned once more, her body growing hot, although he hadn't yet lit the logs. He stood silent for a moment and studied her, from her tumbled hair to her flaming cheeks, to her shawl held out like a shield, to the water that encircled her feet. "You're dripping," he murmured. "Shouldn't you get changed?"

"I-I'll be fine once the fire gets started. I'll dry off quickly."

He sighed. "Go ahead and put on dry clothes. I'll keep my back to you."

Just thinking about changing while Joe was in the cabin

made Grace nervous, but she realized she could climb up and get changed in the loft. True to his word, Joe turned his back and, keeping an eye out to make sure he wasn't peeking, Grace tossed her sopping shawl into the tin basin so she could climb the ladder. Once in the loft, she changed quickly, relieved at the feel of dry clothes on her skin, and then re-braided her hair. By the time she climbed back down, the kindling was crackling welcomingly. Joe squatted beside the fireplace, shivering and rubbing his hands together.

"You need to get dry too," Grace said. "You should change the . . . the rest of your clothes."

"Change into what?"

Joe stood up and faced her, and her mouth went dry at the sight of his bronze chest in the flickering firelight. "Oh, um . . ." She was having trouble putting together coherent thoughts. Perhaps the widow still had some of her husband's old clothes. "I'll see if Miz Burns has anything for you to wear . . ."

He smiled a little. "Think I'd look good in her Sunday best? That is, if she didn't take it with her into town."

"No, I was thinking she might have some . . ." Why was it so hard to talk? "Some shirts or pants. She's a recent widow like Caroline, so maybe . . . I'll go see." Grace had to get away from him. Tearing her gaze away, she scurried up the ladder again to have a look, but she couldn't find any clothes, not even the widow's. All she had was her own buckskin shirt — the shirt Sequoyah had given her in the Ndeh camp. Joe would never get her shirt over his broad . . . strong . . . shoulders . . . She shook her head, trying to clear the thoughts crowding her mind. She was sorry she'd hurt him, but Grace was sure she'd done the right thing in trying to keep him at arm's length for now. She couldn't get into a relationship.

She swallowed, realizing she still hadn't found anything for Joe to wear. Maybe he could wrap himself in a blanket? She pulled the quilt off the feather bed and tossed it down to Joe. "Uh, maybe you can use that until your clothes are dry."

Joe chuckled. "Good idea. Just a moment . . ."

She sat on the bed and waited, trying not to imagine him taking off the rest of his wet clothes only a couple of feet away from her.

"Grace?" Joe's voice floated up to her, making her jump. "You can come down now. I'm decent."

When she peeked down from the loft, Joe stood by the fire, wrapped in the quilt. His shirt and trousers now both dangled from the ends of the hearth, far enough from the flame not to catch fire, but close enough to dry quickly.

Breathing a sigh of relief that he was covered from head to toe, Grace descended.

Joe smiled. "Thanks for the quilt. And the shelter." His gaze went to her hair. "Oh, you braided it." He sounded disappointed. "Wouldn't it dry faster loose?"

"I suppose." Imagining Joe running his hands through her hair unnerved her. She took a breath.

"You have beautiful hair," he said shyly.

"Thank you," Grace whispered.

Her heart began to thump like the rapid rhythms of the Ndeh drums, which only reminded her of dancing with Joe in the moonlight. She swallowed hard. They were alone in a cabin with only a quilt between her and Joe's nakedness . . .

She had to divert the conversation before the sparks flying between them lit a fire more powerful than the one in the hearth, one that burned out of control, but she couldn't rein in her scattered thoughts. Sensible ideas floated just out of reach, to be replaced with memories of Joe touching her, kissing her. Of Sequoyah's gentle teasing, asking if Grace loved him.

Sequoyah. Grace seized that random thought and forced out a question. "H-how is Sequoyah? She and Dahana are now married?" She felt a surge of guilt that she hadn't been in touch with her friend for a while, and a little embarrassed at the abrupt change of subject.

Joe exhaled, seeming relieved too. "No," he said with a frown. "Her father still wants her to marry Tarak, even though she rejected his proposal."

Grace sank onto the sofa, grateful to be off her shaky legs, and Joe settled into the rough-hewn rocker across from her.

"Poor Sequoyah," she said with a sigh. "If she'd admit her love for Dahana instead of keeping it a secret . . ." Grace stumbled to a halt. Couldn't she find a topic that didn't make her think about her relationship with Joe?

He pretended not to notice her hesitation. "Well, she refuses to tell Cheis, and he only wants the best for her. Tarak is, after all, the best warrior." His face twisted into an expression of distaste.

Grace mirrored his dislike of Tarak, but for different reasons. He'd objected to Joe teaching her to be a warrior and continually let them know it.

"But Sequoyah wants to follow her heart," she said quietly, biting her lip.

"I know. She's desperately unhappy. I only hope she doesn't do anything foolish."

"Would Cheis be so upset if she married Dahana?"

Joe shrugged. "I don't know. I doubt she'll be able to ignore her father's wishes."

Her heart ached for her friend. Tarak had staked his horse outside Sequoyah's home, the typical Ndeh proposal. She'd had four days to indicate her acceptance by feeding the horse, but Grace left the Indian camp before Sequoyah had made her choice. She had encouraged Sequoyah to tell her father that she loved Dahana, not Tarak, but evidently her friend hadn't followed her advice. Although, to be fair, Grace hadn't followed her friend's advice either. Sequoyah had told Grace to follow *her* heart and marry Joe . . .

"Grace?" Joe had his head tilted to one side as if waiting for an answer.

"Oh, I'm sorry. Did you say something?"

He looked crestfallen but waved a hand in the air. "Never mind. Must not have been important enough to get your attention."

"I'm sorry. I was thinking about Sequoyah."

"What about her?" Hurt edged his words.

Grace wasn't about to mention her friend's advice. "I wish I could see her again. I really miss her."

"Did . . . did you miss *me*?"

More than he would ever know. But Grace didn't know how to answer his question. All she wanted was to be swept into his arms, but that was dangerous, much too dangerous. Especially now they were alone, with the fire roaring . . . She couldn't meet his eyes.

"Of course I did," she whispered, then in a louder voice added, "I miss everyone — Cheveyo, Cheis . . ."

"I see." Joe pressed his lips into a line.

Grace had no idea how to let him know she cared without igniting the passion between them, but Joe's stiff shoulders and strained face revealed that she had hurt him deeply again.

"I-I meant what I said in the saloon, Joe. All of it."

"Don't toy with me, Grace. This isn't a game for me, like it is for you." He stood and moved toward the door. "I think I'd be better off sleeping out in the rain tonight."

"Wait! Joe, please try to understand." Her voice dropped to a whisper. "I-if I push you away, it's not because I don't want . . ." She tailed off, unsure whether she should finish her thought.

"Grace, much as it pains me, I promise I won't interfere with your quest to find the Guiltless Gang." He looked at her hard. "I intend to keep my word. So if that's the problem —"

"That's not —"

Joe whirled toward her, glowering. "Then what *is* the problem, Grace? You can't stand the idea of . . . of loving me? Of letting me love you back?"

Her breath caught sharply at his words — they cut her to the quick, and she focused on her lap, where she was wringing her hands. He loved her? She could barely breathe. Joe had been honest with her, and she knew he deserved her honesty in return, but still she hesitated.

"Never mind. Your silence is answer enough." Joe reached for the door latch.

"You can't go out there. It's pouring."

"Save your care for someone else," he muttered. "Someone you're willing to be honest with."

"Wait, Joe, please." She cleared her throat. "It-it's not because I can't stand the idea of . . . loving you. In fact, it's *because* of that I'm afraid of being alone here with you."

He wheeled around. "You don't trust me. Haven't I always been honorable? Have I ever done anything to show myself to be untrustworthy?" He was practically shouting, and for a moment, with him gripping the blanket around his body, it was almost comical. If his words weren't so heartbreaking. "You're willing to hide out here and risk your safety to lure an outlaw, but you're afraid of *me*?"

"Not you, Joe. Me!"

He stood staring at her as if she'd hit him with a poker. "What do you mean by that?"

Grace took a breath. "I'm afraid of what might happen if we're alone here together all night. I don't know if I can . . ."

"Wait, are you saying what I think you're saying?" His own breathing seemed to be speeding up. "You're afraid of what you might do?"

Her face burning, eyes fixed on the rag rug by her feet, she whispered, "Outside in the rain when you looked at me . . ." She buried her face in her hands.

"You want to be with me as much as I want to be with you?" Joe's voice was gentle but laced with passion.

She nodded.

"Oh, Grace . . ." Joe crossed the room and knelt beside her. He tucked the quilt around himself tightly but slid one hand out and took hers. "Look at me."

She hesitantly lifted her gaze to meet his eyes. She'd expected he'd think badly of her, but instead the love shining in his eyes warmed her even more than the fire.

"I've been so tangled up in my own feelings, I gave no

thought to . . ." Joe swallowed hard. "I'd never take advantage of your love. I only want to be with you. To . . . to spend time with you."

"I want that too."

"Is it all right if I sit beside you?"

Shyly, Grace nodded and moved over to make room for him on the sofa.

Joe settled beside her and fixed the quilt so he could wrap an arm around her. Grace laid her head on his chest, reveling in the beat of his heart.

"Grace?"

Joe whispering her name sent shivers down her spine, and she tilted her head to meet the heat of his gaze. Her mouth went dry, drier than the sandstorm that had raged earlier, and in the pause between her breaths, he bent and touched his lips to hers. Before she could stop herself, her arms snaked around Joe's neck, pulling him closer, deepening the kiss. She melted against him, and he tightened his embrace.

Suddenly, he broke away with an unsteady laugh. "We'd better confine ourselves to talking, or . . ." His tanned cheeks glowed crimson as his words trailed off. He looked off in the distance and, his words barely a whisper, caressed her shoulder. "If we keep kissing like that, I'll have trouble remembering my promise."

A little ashamed of her eager response, Grace unwound her hands from behind his head and twisted out of Joe's encircling arms. When she moved to stand, he grabbed her hand.

"Don't go. I love holding you, just . . . being close to you." He drew her back toward him. "Please?"

Grace couldn't resist the pleading in his eyes and let him pull her closer in to him again. "But no kissing." She wasn't sure who her stern warning was for — him or herself. She only knew that around Joe she behaved like tinder to a spark. If she wasn't careful, someone would get burned.

CHAPTER 11

Blinding sunlight woke Grace the next morning. In the haze between sleep and waking, rough-hewn walls emerged in her cloudy vision, and she noticed the faint scent of smoke from a dying fire hanging in the air. She needed to get up and help Ma, but she was reluctant to leave this cocoon of comfort. She snuggled closer to the warm body beside her, the arm encircling her. Arm? She wasn't sharing the bed with Abby . . .

Of course not. Grace began to remember. Her sister was —

Her throat tightened, and she struggled to push away the conflicting memories. She had to get back to the light, to the bright sunlight of being with Joe. Through the blur of moisture clouding her eyes, the unfamiliar cabin walls and furniture took shape and she shook her head a little, trying to free herself from the shadows of the past.

Beside her, Joe mumbled something in his sleep and his arm tightened around her. She concentrated on him holding her close. They'd talked late into the night, cuddling by the fire on the sofa, and she had no recollection of drifting off to sleep. What stood out vividly in her mind was the heat of Joe's lips touching hers and her eager response . . .

Her cheeks grew warm, and the desire to touch Joe and kiss him again grew overwhelming. Before her last bit of resolve crumbled, she wriggled out of his embrace, but she sat beside him a moment to watch the rise and fall of his chest under the quilt. She reached over and smoothed back wayward strands of his shoulder-length hair that had fallen over his face. Joe's lips moved, but he didn't wake. Grace smiled. Back in the Ndeh camp, he had been an early riser, but this morning it seemed as if he could sleep through a buffalo stampede. Emboldened, she reached out and stroked the stubble on his cheeks and chin.

Without opening his eyes, Joe captured her hand, brought it to his lips, and pressed a kiss into her palm. Then he entwined his fingers with hers and sat up, the quilt sliding from his upper body. Grace swallowed hard and fought to tear her gaze from his tanned, rock-hard chest.

He scrunched his brows. "You all right?"

His tenderness along with the swirling tangle of grief

and desire inside triggered her to sudden tears. She turned her head so he couldn't see them, but with a gentle finger Joe turned her face toward him. "Did I upset you?" He brushed away the tears with a feather-light touch.

Grace shook her head. The ache in her chest expanded, constricting her breathing.

"Why are you crying?"

Grace's eyes filled with fresh tears. "I-I dreamed I was home again with Ma and Pa and . . ." Her voice came out hoarse and strained. "I just . . . I felt safe for a moment, here with you, but then I remembered . . ."

His eyes filled with compassion, Joe reached for her and drew her into his arms, cradling her head against his chest. Grace allowed the tears to fall as he stroked her hair and murmured soothing words. After her tears were spent, the rhythmic thump of Joe's heart and the evenness of his breathing calmed her. She wanted to stay here forever . . .

But she had a job to do.

She pushed away from his chest and sat up straight. Although her throat was still thick with tears, she tried to make her voice steady. "You . . . you should go soon," she said with a sigh. "I need to be alone here in case the thief shows up."

"Right," he said, and she could tell he was trying to hide disappointment. "I'd better be getting out of here then." He pushed himself off the sofa, turned, and strode toward the fireplace, clutching the quilt around him.

"Joe? I'm sorry. I didn't mean —"

"Didn't mean what?" he replied tightly, grabbing his buckskins from the mantelpiece. "Don't worry, Grace. I know how important your job is to you."

"It's just —"

"I understand. It's fine." Joe's tone was a cross between hurt and upset. He cleared his throat and his gaze seemed to soften a little, the hint of a smile in his eyes. "Uh, fair warning here. I'm going to drop the quilt to put on my pants now."

Grace sucked in a sharp breath and whirled around so her back faced him. When he stamped to the other side of the hearth, she was tempted to peek before he put on his shirt, but she clenched her hands and teeth and willed herself not to look. She only turned when she heard a low mumbled curse escape his lips.

"My shirt's still wet."

"Oh. But it was hanging by the fire all . . . night . . ." Her voice petered out as she saw him, standing in his buckskins, chest bare, staring up at the roof.

"There's a leak in the roof. Rain must have come in all night. It ran down this side of the mantelpiece," he muttered, kicking at the tin bath almost directly beneath his shirt. "Guess that's why this is beside the hearth. It's almost full." He shook his head and looked up at the hole. "Maybe I could come by and fix it for Widow Burns before it gets worse. After you catch your bounty, that is," he added, shooting Grace a look filled with frustration. "If you can bear to have me around town that long."

"Oh, Joe," Grace said, holding out a pleading hand. "It's not that I don't want you around. It's just that I need to —"

"Get revenge."

Grace shook her head. "No. Justice."

"Call it what you will, but I can't help worrying." Joe glanced down. "About you. About your safety. About whether you'll come out of these encounters *alive* . . . I understand why you want revenge — or justice, as you call it. But I'm afraid of what it might do to you."

He looked over at her earnestly, so much care in his eyes that her lower lip began to quiver.

"I really did listen to what you and the Ndeh said. I'm trying not to let darkness overwhelm me." Her voice shook. "Sometimes it's so hard when I'm alone."

Joe swallowed hard. "You don't have to be alone. I've offered to —"

"I know. It's just that every time we're together, I forget about what I need to do."

"Maybe that's just as well?" he said hopefully.

She shook her head. "I can't let anyone else suffer the way I have."

"The sentiment's admirable, Grace, but don't you think that's the sheriff's responsibility?"

"I'm a bounty hunter now. It's my job too. And if that

means I'm also in a position to try and track down the Guiltless and get justice for my family, then all the better." She set her jaw. "The deputy had no men to protect these women. Someone has to do it."

"Why do you think that someone has to be you?" Joe's voice was sharp.

When Grace glowered at him, he raised his hands in surrender. "Before you get all worked up, you should know," he began, stepping closer to her, "I *do* admire what you're doing. But I can't help worrying about you." His voice grew softer as he stood in front of her.

"I'm the best tracker and shot around, thanks to my teacher," Grace murmured. It was hard to concentrate with him so close.

Joe grinned. "I did a good job, didn't I?" Then he sobered. "Sooner or later, though, you could run into someone who's a better shot."

Grace stuck her chin in the air and pretended to be offended, but deep inside she had to admit a fear that one day she just might meet her match . . .

Joe sighed and hung the damp shirt back up away from the leak. "I think I have another shirt out with my other things in the barn." He brushed his lips to hers lightly, sending her head into a spin, then headed for the door. "I'll get going. I'll feed the horses and let Bullet out."

When Grace started to protest, Joe waved a hand. "Least I can do after you took me in during the storm."

After the touch of his lips, she couldn't help wanting him to stay a bit longer. "Well, it's only just dawn. I'm sure we have a little time. While you do that, I'll make breakfast for both of us before you head out to set up camp."

"No need. I have supplies in my saddlebag." Joe's words were stiff and his muscles tense. He was obviously still hurting.

"Least I can do after you helped me through the storm this morning," Grace said with a smile, though her words were laced with emotion.

Joe's brows drew together in a puzzled frown. Then a warm half-smile formed on his lips as he realized she meant her crying spell. "In that case . . ."

By the time he returned, disappointingly wearing a shirt now, she had the meal ready. She set the bowls of hominy on the table, and Joe sank into the chair across from her, his hair still damp from washing at the pump. Grace forced herself to concentrate on dipping her spoon into the bowl. If she kept glancing at Joe, she'd be tempted to forget about breakfast.

He seemed to be avoiding her eyes too. "Mmm. This is delicious, Grace," he murmured. He ate hastily though, and as soon as he scraped the last spoonful of hominy from his bowl, he pushed back his chair. "Thanks for the meal, but I'd better get out of here so I don't scare off your quarry."

She fought back her disappointment. "I don't expect

he'll arrive until after nightfall. All the women said he waited until after dark . . ."

"In that case, I'll go check on the Ndeh. They may need help repairing their *kuugh'as* after last night's storm. But I'll be back to set up camp by sunset."

"Okay."

She stood too, and Joe walked over and tilted her chin up a little with his finger. "Like you said before . . . if I don't leave now, I might find it hard to go at all," he said quietly.

Grace nodded. She wished Joe could spend the day, but he was right — if the outlaw was staking out the cabin and saw a man, he'd move on. "You'll stay hidden when you come back?" she asked reluctantly.

"Don't worry. Remember that great teacher who showed you tracking skills? I think he can sneak up without being heard or seen." Joe grinned, then leaned over and gave her a chaste peck on the cheek.

Hungry for more, she reached up and pulled him closer. She pressed her lips to his, and Joe's arms tightened around her, their kiss deepening. When they finally broke apart, he stared down at her with such love in his eyes that Grace's breath hitched. Placing his hands on her shoulders, he stepped back and swallowed hard.

"If you keep kissing me like that, woman, I will certainly never leave." His words came out unsteadily as he edged backward to the door. His hands fumbled behind his back for the door latch, his longing gaze still on her.

After the cabin door shut behind him, Grace touched one finger to her lips, still feeling the imprint of his mouth on hers. She opened the door and watched as he mounted Paint and rode off into the distance.

*   *   *

The lonely day stretched before Grace. To keep her mind off Joe, she cleaned the stables, exercised the horses, and even polished the saddles, but by lunchtime she had returned all the horses to their stalls. All except Bullet. With clear skies overhead, she left him in the paddock and then headed back to the house.

She had just closed the front door when she heard hoofbeats sound in the distance. Joe wouldn't announce his presence that way, she was sure of it. She was surprised that the thief would arrive in broad daylight, but Grace nevertheless eased the revolver from the holster at her side before she latched the door. She moved to the vantage point she'd picked out the day before, her body tense and alert as she peeked out the window.

Through the trees, she spotted flashes of brown — a horse, mane and tail flying, with a black-coated rider astride. Partway up the hill, the horse slowed and picked its way over the fallen tree limbs from last night's storm. The rider's head was tipped so his hat shaded his face. He had the right build, but she couldn't tell if his features matched Emily's description of Black Coat.

The rider reached the top of the trail and turned his horse toward the cabin. This was not a random stranger passing by; this man obviously knew where he was heading. Straight toward the cabin. Grace's stomach clenched. She hoped her trap would work. If only Joe were around to provide backup. His earlier comment about meeting her match someday only increased her apprehension, and she conjured up memories of other, successful bounty hunts to bolster her courage. She could do this. This man deserved to be taken down. She hadn't come all this way to be scared by a weakling who preyed on lone women.

The man dismounted and turned toward the cabin . . . Grace exhaled hard when she recognized him. It was John Byington, the preacher. She muttered in irritation under her breath. He'd spoil her plans, surely.

Grace slid her gun back into the holster and opened the door. "Reverend. What are you doing here?" Her words sounded unwelcoming, so she quickly added, "It's good of you to check up on me."

Reverend Byington looped the reins over the porch railing and mounted the steps. "I'm actually here to take you back to town. It is much too dangerous for you to be here on your own. I just got word of you coming out here —"

"I have a job to do, Reverend, and I have a plan. I will

be fine. This is the only way I know to flush that thief out of hiding."

The preacher's brow creased. "From what I understand, he's not just a thief. It's not safe for a young girl to be isolated out here."

"Someone has to catch this criminal! The women can't stay in town indefinitely."

Reverend Byington's eyes held a deep skepticism. "That's true, but it's a job for the sheriff."

She folded her arms. "I told you — he has no man power. The posse and all the bounty hunters are busy."

"I admire your dedication to helping others, Grace, but we talked before about being foolhardy —"

"Thanks for your concern, but like I said, I'll be fine."

The preacher lifted his hat and wiped the sweat from his brow.

Grace was reluctant to invite him inside — she needed to send him on his way before dusk, which was approaching fast. And before he scared off her potential target. But how could she refuse him a drink and a rest when he was so hot and dusty? She gestured quickly toward the pump. "Would you like me to draw some water for you and your horse?"

The preacher smiled. "I'd be most grateful."

When Grace handed him the water, he said, "I promised Mrs. Burns that I'd check on the leak in the roof. She worried that the storm might have made it worse."

"Uh . . . it's fine." Grace edged around until she was blocking the entrance. She didn't want him coming in and staying too long tinkering with the roof. "All the water flowed into the tin bath she had there. I've been using the rainwater for washing. It's real handy."

Reverend Byington strode toward her. "Nevertheless, a promise is a promise. I must at least check it with my own eyes."

"Like I said, all is well."

The preacher gave her a curious look before moving past her to open the door. Grace hurried through the door first, suddenly remembering — Joe's shirt was still hanging on the mantelpiece. What would the preacher think of that? She moved in front of it, hoping to block his view. She gestured toward the table and the chair where she and Joe had eaten breakfast.

"Umm, would you like to sit down? Have a cup of tea? I could —" She stumbled to a stop when the preacher glanced over her shoulder, his eyes widening.

"Grace, is that a man's shirt?"

The sternness in Reverend Byington's voice made Grace's heart sink. When his disappointed eyes turned in her direction, a slow burn moved up her neck until her whole face felt aflame. "It's not what you think. Joe got caught in the storm last night and needed to dry his clothes." The words streamed from her mouth faster than the rain had fallen in last night's storm.

The preacher pursed his mouth, and deep worry lines appeared around his eyes. "So Joe spent the night with you?"

"No! Yes . . . Well, not exactly . . ."

"He's keeping you company up here?"

"Not the way you think." Grace hastened to explain. "He's hiding outside as backup, in case I get into trouble. He insisted. But with the storm last night —"

The preacher's frown deepened.

"He needed shelter."

Reverend Byington shook his head. "You know what the Good Book says about staying away from all appearances of evil. It's not wise to court ill repute."

"I'm not. I — we — didn't . . ." Grace hadn't thought her face could get any hotter, but her skin was as scorched as if she were standing inside a roaring fire. Her voice dropped to a whisper. "We didn't do anything wrong."

The preacher exhaled hard. "I know you to be honest, Grace. But you must think of your reputation. If others find out . . ." He tapped a finger against his lip.

"I understand." She kept her gaze fixed on the irregular wood pattern of the floor.

Byington glanced around. "Is he here now?"

"No, he went to the Ndeh camp to see if they needed help. He'll be back by nightfall, keeping a safe distance." In more ways than one.

"Well, it is good to know that Joe will be around

for your protection, at least. But I still wish you would return to town."

"I can't. Not until this man is caught. And frankly, Joe is better backup than the sheriff."

"It's true he can outshoot most men I've met, but still . . ." Reverend Byington's sigh seemed to come from the depths of his soul. "I'm not going to convince you, am I?"

She smiled a little. "No. I can't let Caroline and Emily down. Or Widow Burns, or any of the other ladies." She tried to keep the impatience from her voice. "I don't mean to hurry you along, Reverend, but I'm afraid Black Coat won't come if he sees your horse." She hoped the preacher's visit hadn't already spooked the outlaw.

He chuckled. "Fret not — if he does see it, he'll recognize my horse. Everyone around these parts knows I travel to the remote cabins to call on widows and orphans to be sure they're safe. No worries. I'm not blowing your cover."

Grace hoped he was right.

"Still, seeing as how you're impatient for me to be off, I won't take you up on your offer for tea." Reverend Byington stood and headed for the door, to her relief. He paused, and turned to look at her sternly. "Promise me you won't take any foolish chances."

"I'll do my best."

The preacher went down the porch steps and mounted his horse, tipping his hat. "May God keep you safe. I'll be praying." He clicked to his horse and they started off down the trail.

Though Grace had longed for him to leave, a pool of loneliness swirled inside her as Reverend Byington rode away. She'd been alone in town, but out here with only the sound of the birds and Bullet's occasional snorts, her sense of isolation seemed to increase tenfold. She tried not to think of Joe and the warmth and safety his presence brought.

When trees hid the preacher from view, Grace hurried inside and latched the door. She knew she might have hours to wait, and perhaps even a lonely night to get through. For all she knew, it could be days or weeks before the man showed up. She hoped that wouldn't be the case but decided the best thing to do was to keep busy. She laid the fire, scrubbed the table, and scoured the cooking pots. While she washed her clothes from the night before, she again imagined living here with Joe as husband and wife. They'd care for their horses together and spend their nights by the fire . . .

A movement in the late afternoon shadows outside the window caught Grace's attention. A man — dressed in a black frock coat — crept around the paddock fence, trying to get close to Bullet. Grace gritted her teeth and patted the revolver. Black Coat had arrived. Time to catch her bounty.

Just then the man turned, and their gazes met.

CHAPTER 12

Grace broke eye contact and headed quickly for the door. She opened it wide enough to peer out but kept her gun concealed. Catching sight of her, Black Coat swaggered over.

"I was just admiring that beautiful piece of horseflesh there," he said, motioning over his shoulder with his thumb.

The man's smarmy voice grated on her, and the way he was eyeing her up and down made her furious, but she needed to lure him into her trap. She batted her eyelashes and added honey to her words. "Why, thank you. Can I help you with something, sir?"

"Well, little lady, is yer ma or pa at home? Or are you

the mistress here?" The snide way he asked the question indicated he knew that she was alone.

"Oh, I'm not the owner. I'm just tending her horses until she returns."

"You? You mean your husband's caring for them?"

"Of course." Grace followed her smooth answer with a small laugh, hoping she sounded feminine and fragile enough that he'd consider her easy prey. Behind the door, she tightened her grip on her gun. "He had to ride into town, but he'll be back soon."

The man tipped his hat. "Earl Plimpton, here, ma'am. I apologize for intruding, but my horse injured his leg. I would be mighty obliged if I could let him rest a bit. Wouldn't mind sitting a spell myself." He twisted his hat in his hands as if he were nervous and shy about asking a favor.

If Grace hadn't known he truth, she might have been taken in by his play-acting. She hoped her performance would equal his. Making her voice soft and uncertain, she replied, "I'm not sure my husband would approve of me entertaining strangers in the house." She gestured to her right. "Perhaps you could sit on the porch? I'll bring you a lemonade."

"Well now, that sounds mighty nice, but —" He glanced at the sky. "I'm afeared another storm's coming."

"Oh dear." Grace looked in the direction he pointed. "Do you think so?"

"I know so." Plimpton's voice turned harsh, cruel. "Not the kind of storm you'd expect, though."

He lunged at the door, smashing it into her. Grace crashed onto her backside, cursing under her breath as the revolver flew from her hand and skidded across the floor. She scrabbled for the gun but Plimpton fell heavily on top of her, and her breath whooshed from her body. Her ribs ached from the impact, and the odor of weeks-old sweat mingled with cigar smoke choked her. Pinning her hands against the wooden floor, he smirked down at her.

"So what's a sweet young thing like you doing with a weapon? You don't know how to use it, do you?"

"Why don't you let me show you what I can do with it?" she snarled.

The laughter that burbled from deep in Plimpton's chest chilled Grace to the core, and his lips twisted in an evil grin. "You're gonna show me what you can do, all right — but you won't need a gun."

Tobacco-stained teeth headed for her mouth and Grace jerked her head to one side. Rough stubble raked her skin, and Plimpton growled and grabbed both her wrists with one beefy hand. His head descended again. Gagging and choking, Grace whipped her head from side to side, but he ground his lips and teeth against her mouth. Frantic, she writhed and kicked, trying to dislodge him, but his iron grip on her wrists tightened so much she squealed.

He chuckled. "Now, that is what I like to hear from

a woman." His free hand fumbled for his belt. "Hold still, girl. This won't take long."

Anger surged through her, and Grace clamped her teeth together to prevent another sound from escaping. She twisted her body and managed to wrench one of her hands from his grip. Nails extended, she clawed at his face. He snarled and let go of his belt buckle. With his free hand, he struggled to recapture her wrist, but she flailed her arm, evading him. He emitted a low growl of frustration. Darting a hand under his arm, Grace jabbed him in the eye with her fingers. Plimpton howled and loosened his grip slightly, and she took the opportunity to yank her other wrist away, shoving at his chest, desperate to free herself.

His fist whipped through the air and crunched into her jaw, jarring her teeth and momentarily blackening her vision. Then Plimpton began to tear at her bodice. Though every movement of her head brought waves of pain so intense her stomach roiled, she again scratched fiercely at his face and hammered at him with her fists. Plimpton's fingers closed around her neck, but as they did, one hairy arm brushed past her mouth. She grimaced but then bit down — hard. Plimpton screeched and drew back, and Grace squirmed and bucked, managing finally to tip him to one side. She thrashed to keep him off balance, and Plimpton fought to grab her flailing arms, but she evaded his grip. With one last thrash, gritting her teeth, she managed to smash her knee into his groin.

Plimpton cried out and doubled over on the floor, and Grace shook herself free of him and crawled for the gun. Shaky and with a throbbing head, she stood up and trained her revolver on him as he lay rocking back and forth, his eyes glazed over with pain. She reached down and slid his own gun swiftly from his holster, then stepped back to set it on the table behind her. When Plimpton finally focused on her and her revolver, his eyes widened. He shook his head. "You ain't gonna use that thing, woman."

"You a betting man, Earl? We could bet on that."

With a grimace, Plimpton pulled himself into a sitting position. "Aw, now, there's no call for getting angry. We was just having some fun."

"Fun?" Grace spat out the word.

"So maybe I got a mite rough, but you can't blame a man." The predatory gleam was back in his eyes. "You're so beautiful I had trouble controlling myself." Plimpton pushed himself up on one knee.

"Stay where you are or I'll shoot." Grace barked out the words.

Plimpton stopped for a second and looked at her, holding out a pleading hand. "Let's start over, sugar. I'll take it slow and gentle. I promise I won't do anything you don't want to do."

The man was a superb actor. Grace had to give him that, but his act sickened her. He was lower than a sidewinder and just as slithery.

When he made a move to rise, she snapped, "You move so much as another *inch* and I'll shoot."

With a smarmy smile, Plimpton rocked back onto his heels. "Aw, sweetheart, you don't mean that."

"Try me." Her finger itched on the trigger.

In one swift move, he uncoiled himself and lunged.

Grace fired.

He flew backward, cracking his head on the hearth, and lay on the floor moaning and clutching his arm. Focusing through the black smoke at the end of her gun barrel, Grace prepared for another shot in case he rose.

"The next one's going through your heart."

Behind her, the door banged open so hard it shook the cabin walls.

She jumped and spun around, pointing the revolver at the intruder.

CHAPTER 13

"Grace! Are you all right?" Joe stopped, hands raised, when he spotted the gun.

The desperation in his voice and the concern on his face touched Grace's heart, and she longed to fling herself into his arms, but she knew she had to stay alert. A groan came from the hearth and she whirled, her gun aimed at Plimpton once more.

"What happened?" Joe eyed the man sprawled on the floor. "Is he the one you were after?"

Her lips pinched in a tight line, Grace nodded.

"You shot him?" Joe strode to the hearth where blood was pooling under Plimpton's shoulder.

"We had a tussle."

"What?" Joe looked up, and his hands balled into fists as he took in her disheveled clothes and puffy cheek. He rushed over to her, lifting her chin and tilting it to the light. "He did this?" he said quietly, trailing a finger lightly along her cheek and over the finger marks on her neck. Joe's touch involuntarily set Grace's pulse zinging, but she forced herself to keep her eyes averted and the gun trained on Plimpton.

When his gaze reached her ripped bodice, Joe's jaw clenched. "He didn't —"

"He tried." Her throat had closed so tightly she could barely get the words out. She pushed away memories of Plimpton's hands on her body. The disgusting kiss and his hands tearing at her clothes. Remembering it almost made her retch.

"That bastard. That low-down, dirty bastard." Joe strode toward the hearth, anger in every line of his body. "So help me, I'm going to —"

"Joe . . ." Grace said in a warning voice, though part of her wanted him to beat the man to a pulp.

He swung back his foot and booted Plimpton hard in the rear, and the criminal yowled, clutched at his bloody shoulder, and cowered.

"You *need* a good kick in your —" Joe's foot hovered over the man's crotch.

Plimpton's face twisted in agony and he drew his legs up closer to his body. "No," he whimpered. "Please."

"I already did that," Grace said.

"You did?" Joe turned to her, admiration temporarily sweeping away the murderous look in his eyes.

"That's how I got away."

Joe shook his head, a slight smile on his lips. "Grace Milton, you are one amazing woman."

Grace had a hard time tearing her gaze from his, but Plimpton had fooled her before. She couldn't take a chance he'd do it again. Joe followed her gaze, and his hand went to his own gun.

"Why didn't you shoot him dead? That's what he deserves."

"Don't —"

"Anyone who would do that to an innocent woman doesn't deserve to live." His voice was low and filled with rage now.

Grace stepped closer and laid a hand on his arm. "He's my bounty."

"You'll get paid whether he's dead or alive." His eyes wouldn't leave Plimpton now.

"Joe, please," she said, trying to think fast. "With your bullet in him, they may think I didn't do it."

Shaking with anger, he finally moved his hand away from his gun. "If I had the money, I'd *pay* you the bounty for the privilege of killing this varmint."

"Actually," Grace said, "don't you think it's fitting punishment for him to be brought into town by a woman?"

Joe looked at her and grinned, but the fury didn't leave his eyes. "That will be fun to watch."

"But . . . I can't have you ride in with me."

"What?" He frowned at her.

"I didn't mean it like that," Grace said, hastening to explain. "I only meant if we go together, everyone *will* think you caught him. You don't know how it is, Joe. They treat me like I'm incapable."

Joe stood silently for a moment. "I see. But I don't want to leave you alone with him. What if he tries something else?"

"I don't think he's in any shape to do that, but we'll tie him up tight to be sure."

Joe unholstered his gun and pointed it at Plimpton. "I'll keep him covered while you get the rope."

Grace cleared her throat and gave Joe a look.

"Oh, right. He's your captive. I'll get the rope. But if he so much as moves, shoot him through the heart."

"I think I can handle it," she said with a small smile.

"I know you can, it's just that . . ." The love shining in Joe's eyes made his message clear, but he swallowed hard. "If anything ever happened to you, I wouldn't be able to bear it."

Too choked up to answer, she hoped her own eyes conveyed her appreciation.

* * *

A short while later, they had half-heartedly bandaged Plimpton's shoulder with rags and trussed him tightly to his horse. Grace changed her bodice and packed her belongings while Joe cleaned the bloodstains from the cabin floor and patched the cabin roof.

After Grace locked the cabin, she and Joe rode toward town together in the gathering dusk, and Plimpton shrieked and cursed as his horse bumped along behind. When they reached the end of the trail, Joe slowed and pulled up beside Grace. Bullet shied as Paint brushed against him, but he settled quickly when she talked to him. Joe leaned toward her, and she met him halfway. Their lips touched, but the ugly memory of Plimpton rose in her mind, and she broke away. All she wanted to do was scrub her lips to erase her queasiness.

Joe's glance — half puzzled, half hurt — made her ache inside. She needed to explain, but not here and not now. And she knew it wouldn't be long before her passion for Joe outweighed any bad memories of Black Coat.

With a curt wave, Joe dug in his heels and galloped ahead. "See you in town," he called over his shoulder, a smile returning to his lips now. "I want to be there for the show."

Grace waited until she could no longer see the puffs of dust billowing behind Paint, then she emerged from the tree line and followed at a sedate pace, with Plimpton and his horse still following behind.

When she reached Main Street, Emily came running toward her, shouting her name.

"You got him!" the little girl called excitedly. "That's the bad man who hurt Ma!" She turned and ran back down the street, yelling for her mother.

Caroline came running to the doorway of the saloon. Across the street, some of the other widows hurried from the boarding house. They pointed and cheered as they saw Grace's cargo, with Emily's "hurrahs" being the loudest of all. Further down the street, Grace spied Joe leaning against a post outside the saloon. He winked, but rapidly resumed the look of a casual bystander.

When she dismounted at the sheriff's office, Caroline rushed over and took her hand. "Thank you. Oh, thank you. You don't know what this means to me." She threw a loathing glance at the man slumped over the saddle of the other horse.

But Grace did understand. Her experience hadn't been as horrific as some of the widows', but she'd never forget the sickening stench of Plimpton, his repulsive body on hers, the terror of being trapped, and his nauseating touch. Even now she shuddered, and disgust made her hands clumsy as she untied the ropes that bound Plimpton to his saddle. The last rope slipped from her grasp, and he plummeted to the ground. She made no move to stop his fall. He screeched when he landed on his side.

The sheriff stepped out into the late afternoon sunlight

and blinked at the crowd surrounding Grace. "What's all this commotion?"

"She caught the bad man who hurt Ma!" Emily's shrill voice rose over the chatter.

The sheriff's gaze darted from Plimpton to Grace and back again. "You didn't go after him all by yourself?"

"Yes, she did," Emily piped up again.

"Deputy Clayton said there was no one else available to do it," Grace reminded him curtly.

"I'm sure he didn't mean for *you* to go after him." The sheriff hoisted Plimpton to his feet, then gave Grace a stern look. "That was a foolish and dangerous thing to do."

Grace glared at him. "I'd say it was more dangerous to leave a man like that at large."

"She's right." One of the women moved to Grace's side and put an arm around her. "You should be thanking her for her bravery."

"I'm impressed by her bravery, but she could have been hurt or even killed. Chasing criminals is no job for a woman." He turned to Grace. "And especially not for a young girl like you."

She clenched her fists at her sides and tried to keep the irritation from her voice. "I've caught three criminals in the past few days. I think I've proved my skills."

"Three?"

"Talk to Deputy Clayton in Tombstone. He'll tell you I'm a seasoned bounty hunter. I took down a criminal as notorious as Doc Slaughter and I aim to get the rest of the Guiltless Gang too."

"That was you who shot Slaughter?" The sheriff's eyebrows rose. "Heard it was some slip of a girl," he murmured, shaking his head. "But you stay away from the Guiltless Gang. One stroke of luck doesn't make you experienced enough to capture them"

Emily frowned at the sheriff. "Grace is the best bounty hunter ever. She'll get that gang, and I'm gonna help her."

Caroline pulled her daughter quickly to her side. "Emily, I don't think —"

"It's all right," Grace assured her. "Emily's doing a wonderful job of studying the wanted posters," she said, leaning down and resting a hand on the girl's shoulder. "She's keeping an eye out for them in town, and she'll tell me if she spots one. But that's all — right, Emily?"

Caroline smiled indulgently. "I'm sure she'll do a fine job with that. She's very observant."

The sheriff headed for his office, a moaning Plimpton in tow. "Guess you'd best come along, young lady, and get your reward." He inspected Plimpton's bandage. "Then I'll send for the doc . . ."

"No rush for that," Grace heard one of the women mutter.

A chorus of thanks and cheers awaited her when she emerged a short while later. The widows all clustered around her. Many of them tried to press some money into her hands, but she waved them away. The last to leave was Mrs. Burns. With tears in her eyes, she hugged Grace and handed her a gold piece for caring for the horses. She tried to refuse, but the widow pressed it into her palm and squeezed her fingers around Grace's.

"You use that toward catching that gang. It's a shame when a young girl has to do a job our men should be doing, but someone has to keep this town safe, and to me you're more than capable. You've proved that, young lady."

Emily sidled up to Grace as the widow left to head for her cabin. "You'll get all those outlaws, won't you, Grace?" She gazed up at her with adoring eyes.

"I hope so. I certainly hope so. Where's your mother?" Grace was anxious to find Joe, but she had something she wanted to do first.

"She had to go back to work."

"Let's go find her."

They found Caroline scurrying back and forth in the boarding house, her arms full of dirty dishes. Grace helped her clear the tables and then handed Emily's mother some money.

"What's this?"

"I couldn't get your horses back," Grace said, "and this won't cover your losses, but it should be enough for tickets to get back East."

When Caroline shook her head, Grace whispered, "This is no place for Emily. I want her to be safe." Visions of her sister Abby brought a lump to her throat. "I'd like to give it to you, but if you can't accept it, then think of it as a loan. You can repay me after you get back home. Just see that you're on the next train out of town."

Tears sprang to Caroline's eyes and she threw her arms around Grace. "You've been a godsend. I will never be able to thank you."

"The only thanks I want is knowing that you're both safe."

Caroline's smile lit up the dark room, and she bent down to hug her daughter. "We're going home, Emily. Back to Nanny and Pappy. And uncles and aunts and cousins . . ."

Emily danced around and then reached out and grabbed Grace's hand. "You're coming with us, aren't you, Grace?"

She opened her mouth to correct her, but Caroline gave her a warning glance over Emily's head. "We'll see, honey," she said to her daughter. "Grace has some family back East, so maybe she'll visit them and come see us too."

"You should come when we go! Then we can all go on the train together." Emily looked at her mother. "When do we leave?"

"As soon as we can. When the next available train comes through town, we'll be on it. Thanks to Grace."

"Can we get our tickets now, Ma, please?" Emily tugged at her mother's hand.

Caroline looked at the pile of dishes and her shoulders sank, but then she straightened and lifted her chin. "Sure. The dishes will wait. Let's hurry before they close for the night. We wouldn't want those tickets to get sold out."

Emily held out her other hand to Grace. "Will you come get your ticket too?"

"I'll go tomorrow," she said. Lying to the girl made Grace uncomfortable, but she had no choice. "Umm, right now I have to meet a friend who's waiting for me."

"All right." Emily skipped away beside her mother, and at the door of the boarding house she stopped and waved. Grace waved back, and Caroline smiled and mouthed *thank you.*

As she walked to the saloon, Grace blinked back tears. She'd tried so hard not to get attached to her, but somehow the girl had wormed her way into her heart. She would miss Emily's cheerful smile and constant chatter. With her and her mother gone, the town would seem lonely and empty. And Joe would soon head off too . . .

He sauntered toward her just as she reached the saloon, his smile melting her heart. "Quite the heroine, aren't you? Care for some dinner? My treat."

Grace smiled back and nodded. "Some of that reward money should be yours."

"No, the criminal was already captured when I arrived."

He held out his arm and she took it as they went into the saloon.

"Why so glum?" Joe asked as they made their way to a table. "Thought you'd be happy — you captured another bounty."

Grace waved a hand to indicate she wasn't ready to talk yet. Not until she could do it without crying.

Joe held up a bottle of sarsaparilla. "Okay. Well, a nice meal and some good company should cheer you up." He smiled and poured the soda into a glass and slid it across the table, then went to order their meals.

After she'd eaten, Grace leaned forward. "I didn't get to ask you before, but how were things in the Ndeh camp? And how is Sequoyah?"

"The storm caused some damage, but by the time I left things had been fixed." A pained expression crossed his face. "Trouble's brewing with Sequoyah and her father though."

"Oh no!" Grace had encouraged Sequoyah to follow her heart and marry Dahana, but now she wondered if that had been the best advice for her friend. "Is she all right? What is she planning to do now?"

Joe pinched his lips together for a moment before answering. "I'm not sure. I'm afraid she's going to do something rash."

"Like what?"

"She was very secretive when I asked her that. And that's not like Sequoyah. I planned to ride back there after dinner . . ."

"Maybe she'd talk to me." If Sequoyah defied her father and rejected Tarak, she'd need an ally. "Joe?"

"Hmm?" He seemed lost in his thoughts. Shaking his head, he focused his attention on Grace again.

"Would you mind if I ride to the Ndeh camp with you? I'd love to see Sequoyah again, and it sounds as if she needs a friend, someone who understands her love for Dahana and supports her."

Joe smiled broadly. "I'd like that. The Ndeh would love to see you, and you're right, Sequoyah does need someone to confide in. She told me today how much she misses you." He pushed back his chair and stood. "We should get on the road, then."

"I just need to get my things and check out of my room."

"Why don't you do that, and I'll get the horses from the stable."

"Sure, thank you," Grace said. "They should be fresh enough now for the ride."

Gathering up her belongings, she wrapped the precious picture of her family in some clothing, packed it away in her bag, and hurried downstairs and through the saloon. But as she neared the doors, Emily rushed in like a whirlwind, almost knocking Grace over. She reached out one hand to steady the girl.

"Emily? What are you still doing out?"

"Oh, Grace! I've been looking everywhere for you."

Her face was flushed red, and she was panting. "Come quick!"

"What's the matter?"

Emily grabbed Grace's free hand and dragged her through the door. "He was there. At the station house."

"Who?"

"The man from the wanted poster. Hurry!"

CHAPTER 14

"Are you sure?" Grace hurried to keep up with Emily.

"It's the man with little holes all over his face," she said, poking her cheeks with her fingers. "And he has those mean eyes and that funny-looking hair here." Emily stopped so abruptly Grace almost ran into her as the little girl rubbed her fingers on her chin. "Not a lot. Only a little."

"A scraggy beard?"

"Yes, yes."

And pockmarked skin. One of the Andersen twins, and Grace knew exactly which one. Wyatt "Iron Eyes." Bile rose in her throat as she thought of his part in her family's murder. Grace swallowed hard at the memory of Abby's helpless body lying on the ground.

"Grace? Grace?" Emily tugged hard at her hand. "What's wrong? Are you sick?"

Yes, she was sick. Nauseous with the gut-wrenching memory of Andersen's uncaring face.

"He'll get away if you don't hurry!" Grace strode quickly after the girl, whose mousey-blonde braids bounced up and down as she rushed along. In her mind, Emily's impatient braids and features faded into Abby's and waves of anger swamped Grace, almost making her choke. Abby would never again run and play. But Emily was alive and well, and Grace aimed to keep her that way. She'd see to it that the Andersen twins never harmed another innocent child. She pushed away all thoughts but capturing the snake who'd killed her baby sister. As soon as she spotted Andersen, she'd send Emily back. Her mother would be unhappy to know the girl was still out and would surely expect her daughter to be at home when she returned from work.

Finally they reached the railway station, only to find it deserted.

"He's gone," Emily said, dismayed.

"You're sure it was him?" She had to ask, but the little girl nodded adamantly.

All the adrenalin shooting through Grace's body plummeted, leaving her drained. The rush to the station combined with all the tensions of the day — her aching muscles from fighting off Plimpton, her swirling emotions from being around Joe, and now coming so close to finding Andersen . . . She slumped against a wooden post, and sparks of pain radiated from her jaw where Plimpton had backhanded her. If Emily hadn't been with her, she would have been tempted to collapse.

"I'm sorry, Grace."

"We'll find him, Em," she said reassuringly, though she had no idea how. Had he been enquiring about train tickets? Did he plan to leave town? Or were his motives more sinister? The posters in the sheriff's office had said the Andersen twins were wanted for several train robberies. They could be planning a heist . . . If only she could talk to the stationmaster to find out what Andersen had been asking about, but the cage over the ticket window was locked. No one was in sight.

Emily pulled away from Grace. "I tried so hard to be a good bounty hunter. I really did." She sighed. "I followed him and listened to him, but when I went to find you, he must have got away."

"You followed him? And listened in?" She put her hands on the girl's shoulders. "That was very, very dangerous."

"I know. I tried to be brave like you said."

Grace shook her head. She'd lecture Emily about that later. Right now she needed any information she could get. "Tell me everything he did and said. Whatever you remember."

Emily brightened. "I did a good job then, didn't I?"

Grace hesitated. "I'm sure you did, but next time you need to be more careful."

"I *was* careful. I hid over there so he couldn't see me." She pointed to a stack of crates a few feet away.

"I'm glad you hid," she said, trying to keep the impatience from her voice. "So tell me everything you saw."

"Better — I'll show you what he did." Emily raced to the shadowy side of the station and hid behind some wooden barrels. She peeked over them a few times, tipped an imaginary hat low over her eyes, and swaggered toward the ticket counter, constantly glancing over her shoulder. She stopped twice, pretending to lower a bandana from her mouth and spit out wads of tobacco. Grace hid her smile. The girl was definitely observant. If Andersen knew how closely he'd been watched, he might have been more careful. Emily stopped before approaching the ticket counter. She glanced around several times before adjusting the "bandana" and tilting the "hat brim" even lower. Then in a low gruff voice she demanded, "I need a ticket for . . ."

She spun quickly toward Grace. "I didn't hear what he said then."

Disappointment surged through her. So close. At least she knew he'd been enquiring about a ticket.

"But then they got in a big argument," Emily continued. "The ticket man yelled, 'I can't give you what I ain't got.'"

"Did you hear anything else they said?"

Emily's face fell. "No, I ran to get you."

"I know." Grace tried to smile. "You did a great job. I'll talk to the ticket master in the morning."

The sun had already set. She needed to get Emily home. "Let's head back. Your ma will be worried." So would Joe, she now realized. In her eagerness to track down Andersen, she'd forgotten all about meeting him at the stables.

"Ma won't worry. I told her I'd be with you."

They walked back toward the boarding house, Emily hurrying to keep pace with Grace's longer stride.

Grace turned to her young friend as they walked. "Did your ma get your tickets?"

Emily nodded. "We bought our tickets, but no train will be coming through for five days. That's what the man told Ma."

"But a train comes through every day."

"Not this week. They're fixing the tracks somewhere down the line."

So the Andersens wouldn't have any trains to hold up until then either. She doubted that they'd loiter here in town while they waited. They must have a hideout somewhere nearby. Her best bet would be to wait and ambush them if they tried to board the train — but how could she find out if the next one was the train they planned to hit?

Excitement began to build inside her. She had five days. A chance to plan something, to stop the Andersen twins.

A chance to catch more of the Guiltless Gang at last. But she'd need to think about her trap carefully. She would talk to the station master and find out what train would interest the Andersens most — useful cargo, precious goods. Then she'd be waiting.

Finally they reached the boarding house. Grace patted Emily on the back. "Go in and find your ma. It must almost be your bedtime."

The girl made a face and looked like she was about to protest, but instead she flung her arms around Grace and hugged her tightly, then she turned and marched toward the front door.

Grace couldn't help smiling, but her face sobered as Joe came racing toward her.

"Grace! Where have you been? I was worried something had happened to you."

"I went to the railway station with a little girl I've . . . befriended, I guess."

"What?" Disbelief added a sharp edge to his voice. "We should have set off for the camp before it got dark, but I didn't want to leave without you."

"I'm sorry." She glanced around to be sure no one was in hearing distance, then she leaned closer to Joe and whispered, "Emily thought she saw one of the Guiltless Gang at the station."

He frowned. "Surely you weren't foolish enough to go chasing after him alone on the whim of a young girl?"

Grace drew back. "I should just let him get away?"

"This town does have a *sheriff*," Joe pointed out.

"A sheriff who's too busy to keep the widows in these parts safe."

"I'm sure he'd make capturing a gang member a top priority." Joe's voice was placating, but his eyes were stern. "You need to give up this vendetta before you get hurt."

She drew herself up. Grace didn't want to argue with Joe, but she wouldn't let those evil Andersen twins go free.

"Grace, I've told you, I care about you. I couldn't bear it if you got hurt."

"I plan to be careful." The stiffness of her words matched the straightness of her back.

Joe shook his head, exasperated. "Remember what happened today?"

"I caught him, didn't I?"

"Members of the Guiltless Gang aren't petty criminals."

"You consider that rapist a petty criminal?"

"That's not what I meant. This gang member you're tracking is a *seasoned* criminal. He has accomplices. You're inexperienced, and you're working alone."

"I've caught everyone I've gone after so far."

"And look at you." He gestured to her swollen face. "You were lucky to escape today."

"That was not luck, Joe. It was skill." Grace brushed past him. "I need to buy more bullets before the company store closes."

She stalked across the street and Joe followed her quickly. "Grace, I'm not doubting your abilities. I only want to —"

She shoved open the door and let it fly shut, cutting off Joe's words. Several men jumped as the door banged, but after eyeing her and apparently deciding she was harmless, they resumed their conversation.

"Anyway, this squaw comes in here today . . ." one of the men said. "And she was a looker." He glanced over at Grace and then dropped his voice to a whisper.

The men around him sniggered.

Joe banged through the door and hurried up to her. "Grace," he pleaded. "Think about what you're doing." He grabbed her arm, but she shook him off.

"I know what I'm doing."

The men stopped their conversation to watch. One of them called out, "Looks like you been keeping her in line, son."

"What?" Joe wrinkled his brow.

The man indicated Grace's red and swollen cheek.

Joe planted his feet wide. "That's not from me," he said through clenched teeth.

"She been cheating on you, eh?"

Grace laid one hand on Joe's arm and flipped her other hand in a dismissive gesture, indicating that he should ignore the taunts. No sense in turning those foolish remarks into a duel. She stepped up to the counter and requested her bullets, but the other man wasn't about to let it drop.

"Best thing to do when they stray, son, is to get your own back. Plenty of painted ladies here in town'd be happy to ease yer pain."

His neighbor elbowed him. "He might like that little Injun squaw, from the look of him. She was dressed like one of them Apaches." He shook his head. "Thought General Crook rounded up all them troublemakers and shipped 'em outta here. Hope we ain't got renegades up in the mountains."

Beside her, Joe's muscles tensed. Grace tightened her grip on his arm and shot him a warning glance. She paid for the bullets with some of her reward money and turned to go.

"Take my advice, son," the man called after them. "You can grab one of them squaws for free. Teach that little lady a lesson."

As soon as they reached the street, Joe exploded. "They degraded you and the Ndeh women with that filth. I should have called them out . . ." He stopped, thinking about something suddenly. "What were they talking about when they said an *Apache*" — Joe spat out the hated word for Ndeh — "came in today? And a *woman?*"

Grace stopped. "That worried me too. None of the Ndeh would take a chance of being caught in town, would they?" *Unless* . . . She nibbled at her lower lip.

Joe's aggressive expression changed to a worried look. "They mostly send me for supplies, which I just brought them. And they'd certainly never let a woman come into town because of men like that." He jerked a thumb over his shoulder. "We'd better get to the camp and make sure everything's all right." He reached out for Grace's hand and they rushed to where their horses were waiting.

As they mounted, Grace said slowly, "You don't think it was —"

"Sequoyah?" Joe finished her thought with a grim look on his face. "I was afraid she'd do something reckless, but I hope she wouldn't be so imprudent."

"I hope not too," Grace said, "but we'd best find out."

They turned their horses in the direction of the Ndeh village and galloped off into the twilight.

CHAPTER 15

Grace and Joe spurred their horses faster in the bright moonlight and finally came to a stop at the edge of the Ndeh encampment. Glowing campfire shined on a group of women shuffling in a circle surrounded by men, and Grace's heart ached as she remembered doing that same dance with Joe alone in the dark soon after she'd first arrived at the Ndeh camp. A feeling of warmth and acceptance flowed over her, as if she were coming home — but that word also brought waves of pain crashing through her. Ma, Pa, Abby, Daniel, Zeke . . . Her soul cried out for the cabin that had once been a haven, but now was only ashes. The Ndeh had helped to heal some of those raw, gaping wounds. These people had surrounded her with kindness, caring, gentleness. For a moment, she and Joe sat side by side astride their horses, watching the graceful movements, lost in the melodic chants.

In many ways Grace's spirit pulled her to these people, this way of life. If she didn't have this drive to get justice for her family's murder and to stop other such crimes happening, she could imagine being a part of the tribe, belonging the way Joe did to this adopted family. Cheis had offered to adopt Grace too, so that she and Sequoyah would be blood sisters. And Joe would be a blood brother? She swallowed. Her feelings for Joe in no way resembled those for a brother . . .

"All seems to be well," he said beside her. "If Sequoyah were missing, they wouldn't be dancing. Want to join them?"

Grace was still too shy to take part in the dances, but when Joe dismounted and took her hand, she melted.

"Please?"

"Not in the group. Can we . . . can we dance here?"

Joe smiled and helped her slide from Bullet's back. "Even better. A chance to be alone with you."

A bubble of joy floated up inside of her and grew until it filled her so full she thought she'd burst. She pushed aside all her worries, her vendetta with the Guiltless Gang, her fears for Sequoyah. Alone in the dark, with the distant drum pounding a steady, syncopated beat that echoed the excitement of her heart, Grace faced Joe and began the shuffling steps of the dance. She let the rhythm carry her away and moved her body in time with the music. Joe had his eyes closed as he swayed with her, and when he opened them, the moonlight revealed they were awash with love.

"Oh, Joe," she whispered.

He faltered, stopped dancing, and stared at her. Grace stumbled to a halt and gazed back. When he held open his arms, she moved into them as if under a spell. Safe in his encircling arms, she laid her head on his chest, feeling the rapid beat of his heart. The fast pitter-patter of her own was like bird wings beating, struggling to fly free. Here, surrounded by trees, a canopy of stars overhead, the scent of pine mingling with the smoke from the fire, Grace felt warm and content and loved. Peace enveloped her and it seemed there was only this moment. She and Joe alone together in the universe where nothing else intruded, nothing else mattered. She tilted her head up and admired his rugged profile in the moonlight, but when his eyes met hers again, she was suddenly lost — drowning in a sea of emotions she'd never felt before, strange conflicting feelings she couldn't name.

"Grace?"

His whisper set off an uproar of emotion. All she wanted was to be close to him, to hold him and never let go — for everything else to disappear until only one thing was left. Joe. Only Joe. She wanted to capture this moment, to keep it with her forever, to stretch it to eternity. She wished the nightmares of the past and the vengeance of the future could never interfere again.

When Joe's lips met hers, she twined her arms around his neck and kissed him with every fiber of her being, with her heart and soul. The softness of his kiss deepened, and Grace met the deepening pressure with passion. She gave herself up to it with complete abandonment, letting her lips convey the message that burned inside. She loved Joe and wanted to be with him not only this moment, but always.

He pulled back and said again shakily, "Grace?"

Again torrents of desire were set coursing through her blood. Though a small voice warned she was playing with fire, Grace whispered back, "Yes." And her body echoed that desire. Yes, yes, yes.

Joe's voice was husky. "Maybe we shouldn't . . ." His words were unsteady, but his fingers were sure as he stroked her jawline and trailed a finger down her neck. Grace had never wanted anything, anyone with such a fierce desire. Inside she burned brighter than the campfire in the distance. She leaned her body against his and he gathered her closer, tightening his arms around her until she was pressed against the length of his body.

"I don't want to stop," she answered in a whisper.

When their lips met again she ran her fingers through Joe's hair and slid them around the back of his neck, pulling him closer . . .

A rustling in the bushes behind them made them jump apart.

They turned to see Sequoyah emerging from the trees. She was almost right beside them before she realized they were there. A small, startled squeak escaped her lips, but she quickly clapped one hand over her mouth and the other to her heart.

"Joe? Grace?" Sequoyah whispered. "You scare me. Very much!"

"We're sorry," Grace whispered back, her own heart beating as rapidly for a different reason. If Sequoyah hadn't approached when she did, Joe and she might have . . . Her face flushed.

"What you are doing here?" Sequoyah asked.

Grace tried to concentrate on the conversation, but her mind was too full of thoughts of Joe, his hands on her body. They'd stepped apart, but his arm was still around her shoulders, and the warmth of it sent sparks of desire coursing through her.

"We're, umm . . ." Her mind went blank. She couldn't remember why they were here, and she couldn't form a coherent sentence, but she didn't have to worry. Sequoyah took over the conversation after glancing from one to the other. "Joe — he find you, yes? And you are . . ." At a loss for words, she stuttered to a stop. "I not know the word."

"Together?" Joe suggested, glancing down at Grace as though he was unsure.

"Yes, yes, that is what I try to say." Sequoyah beamed at both of them. "Grace, you are back to stay?"

Her friend's words penetrated the fog inside her mind. No, she wasn't back to stay. Real life came crashing back in. She had a gang to find, a mission to complete, and she'd almost lost her way in Joe's arms. If he'd asked her then to give up her quest, she would have agreed to anything. Anything at all — and she almost had. Her cheeks burned hotter at that thought. Grace realized that both Joe and Sequoyah were staring at her, waiting for an answer. An answer she couldn't give. She fumbled for words. "Umm, it's so good to be back. To see you again." She frowned, remembering their concerns. "Are *you* all right? I've been worried about you. Joe said —"

"I am fine," Sequoyah said stiffly, then darted a worried glance over her shoulder.

"If everything is all right, why are you sneaking away from the dance?" Joe asked. Then light dawned in his eyes and he glanced around. "Dahana is around here too, isn't he?"

Sequoyah started to shake her head, but stopped when Dahana stepped from the bushes off to their right. He moved to Sequoyah's side, but she edged away.

"The two of you wanted some time alone?" Joe smiled a little and drew Grace closer to his side. "I can understand that, but Sequoyah, what about your father? I thought —"

"I no care what he say." She lifted her chin defiantly.

Dahana was looking over at her with admiration and love, but at her change in stance, a worried frown creased his brow.

Grace reached out a hand to her friend. "Maybe we should talk alone. Just you and me."

Sequoyah looked reluctant, but after a second she put her hand in Grace's and allowed herself to be pulled a short distance away.

"What's going on? Joe said you refused Tarak. Have you told your father that you love Dahana?" Grace asked.

Sequoyah's face turned stony. "Father very angry. Want me to marry Tarak, but he no understand I love Dahana." Her face softened as she said the last three words, and her eyes shone. "We be together," she said with a smile, referencing what Joe had just said about him and Grace.

"But what about your father?"

Sequoyah sighed. "I cannot do what he want."

"So what *are* you going to do?" Grace said, looking at her friend with concern.

Sequoyah refused to meet her eyes. "We find a way. Me and Dahana."

"Meeting him in secret will not be enough, and if your father expects you to marry Tarak . . ." She sighed. "It could be a problem. Sequoyah, I'm worried about you. What will happen if you don't obey your father?"

"Do not worry, Grace. We be fine."

Grace wasn't so sure. Defying Cheis and meeting in

secret couldn't go on forever. Sooner or later they'd be caught. And then what? Sequoyah glanced at Dahana and Joe, who were staring intently at them and also speaking in low voices.

"I go to Dahana right now," Sequoyah said, then grasped Grace's hand. "You stay with me in my *kuugh'a* tonight?"

Grace smiled. "I'd like that." It seemed so long since she and Sequoyah had spent time together, even though only a few months had passed.

"You are good friend," Sequoyah said, reaching over to embrace her. Grace smiled and returned the hug tightly.

"Joe and I will care for the horses, then I'll meet you back at the camp."

Once again, Sequoyah avoided her gaze. "Yes."

Something odd was going on, but Grace wasn't sure what. She couldn't help feeling uneasy as Sequoyah returned to Dahana's side, whispering quietly but urgently as they walked away, their heads bent close together.

Joe stood waiting beside the horses, and as she remembered what they were doing before they were interrupted, she felt prickles of embarrassment crawl up her neck. She tried to keep her tone neutral, to not let her out-of-control feelings take over again. "Sequoyah says she'll meet me at her *kuugh'a* after we get the horses settled for the night."

Joe nodded and handed her Bullet's reins, glancing after their friends with a concerned look on his face.

They walked in silence to the pasture, though the ground around them still rumbled with drumbeats. The chanting from the fireside grew fainter as they climbed the hill to the place where he had first kissed her that starry night. It was only a few months ago, but it seemed almost a lifetime. Joe, too, must have been remembering, because he glanced at the spot where they'd been sitting when that moment happened, and his Adam's apple bobbed up and down as he swallowed.

It was also the place she'd left him sleeping alone, riding away on her quest.

Now it was Grace who had to swallow hard. That had been the most difficult thing she'd ever done. Would she have to do it again? Was there a way to keep Joe in her life *and* complete her mission?

"Grace?" Joe's hesitant voice interrupted her thoughts. "About earlier." He cleared his throat. "I'm sorry I got carried away. I understand if you can't trust me again."

She raised a hand. "No. It was my fault too."

"Maybe we shouldn't . . . Maybe it would be better not to . . ." The crimson that stained Joe's cheeks was visible even in the moonlight. "It's hard being around you and not touching you, but . . . I don't want to lose your trust, and I don't want you to do something you'd regret and have you end up hating me."

"I could never hate you." Grace drew in an unsteady breath. At the thought of not touching Joe, not being cradled in his arms, not . . . emptiness swept through her, a sense of loss so deep that it took her breath away. But maybe Joe was right. One of these times they'd do something they might both regret — after all they weren't betrothed yet. She flushed at thinking of the word *yet*. She needed to keep her mind on her goal.

"You're thinking about revenge again, aren't you?" Joe's voice came from far away. "Your face hardens, your jaw tenses . . ." His tone held a deep sadness. "If you could just let it go, we could —" He stopped speaking when Grace held up a hand, but he continued to shake his head.

She turned and forced herself to walk away toward the pasture. "Let's get the horses settled for the night."

The other horses nickered in delight when she and Joe turned Paint and Bullet loose in the enclosure.

She and Joe headed back to the camp without saying much more to one another. The dancing had quieted and they made their way to separate *kuugh'as* with only a tentative goodnight. Grace found Sequoyah waiting outside her tent, but she didn't seem in the mood to talk; she said she was tired. Grace was a little hurt at her friend's lack of interest in a conversation, but they'd have plenty of time to talk things through in the morning, and as she lay near Sequoyah as she breathed into sleep, Grace felt the same bond, the same closeness she had when she was last with the Ndeh. She really did feel more at home in the Ndeh camp than she did in town.

The others didn't know that she and Joe had arrived tonight, but she looked forward to them surrounding her and welcoming her back in the morning. She was one of them. Grace drifted off to sleep imagining staying here with Joe forever.

* * *

She woke suddenly before dawn and lay still for a moment, uncertain where she was. No crash of glassware or stamp of boots. As her eyes adjusted to the darkness, she could see the stars through the hole in the thatch overhead and she remembered — the *kuugh'a*. The Ndeh camp. A sense of peace flooded over her. Even though soldiers hunted the Ndeh and they often needed to keep their presence a secret, a calmness pervaded their daily life.

Grace took a deep breath of the clean, fresh air, so different from the heavy clouds and stench of smelting that hung over Bisbee. There, the land had been almost stripped of trees, but here in the hills around the camp, the crystal-clear air and soft night-bird songs began to lull her back to sleep. To hear that and the sound of Sequoyah's gentle breathing beside her . . .

Grace pushed herself up on one elbow, listening intently. *Sequoyah?* The air inside the wickiup was still, and she looked around in the darkness, holding her breath. She reached out a hand, but no. Nothing. Sequoyah was gone. Grace sat up and threw off the deerskin blanket.

Where was she? It was too early for the women to start cooking. Had her friend slipped out to spend the night with Dahana? Grace slid her feet into the moccasins Sequoyah had given her last night. If she'd fallen asleep in Dahana's *kuugh'a*, she needed to return before anyone in the village discovered them.

Grace slipped through the darkness toward Dahana's *kuugh'a*. How could she wake them without disturbing any of the neighbors? She softly whistled one of the birdcalls Sequoyah had taught her. When that brought no response, Grace lifted the buffalo hide at the door enough to toss a few pebbles into the wickiup, but only silence greeted her.

She disliked invading their privacy, but she couldn't let Sequoyah be shamed in front of her whole band. Keeping her eyes averted, she pushed aside the buffalo hide and stepped inside. "Sequoyah?" she whispered.

When she got no answer, she glanced around as her eyes adjusted to the darkness. The *kuugh'a* was empty.

Shock and fear rippled through Grace. What had Sequoyah done?

* * *

A slow, sleepy smile crossed Joe's face and he held up his arms, inviting her to join him. She could tell he was still half in slumber, and any other time she would have found that invitation very hard to resist, but right now she had to wake him up.

"Joe," she whispered desperately as she held open the flap of his *kuugh'a*, "Sequoyah's missing. Dahana's gone too."

Joe sat up, rubbing his eyes and looking confused. "What? How do you know?"

"She wasn't in the *kuugh'a* when I woke up, so I went to Dahana's to warn her dawn was coming, but it was empty."

Joe tensed. "You're sure?" His deerskin blanket tumbled to the ground as he jumped to his feet. "Are their horses still here?"

"I didn't check."

Grabbing his shirt, Joe slid it over his head and Grace still couldn't help admiring his torso, but he quickly shoved his feet into his boots and took her hand. "Let's go see."

Hand in hand, they rushed up the hill. Joe whistled and Paint came running, Bullet following close on his heels.

But neither Sequoyah's nor Dahana's horse were in the enclosure.

CHAPTER 16

Grace's heart sank.

"Where could they have gone?"

"I don't know, but we need to follow them while the trail's still fresh," Joe said, jumping the fence. "Can you go grab our saddlebags while I saddle up the horses?"

She nodded and raced off, wondering how much of a head start Sequoyah had. No wonder her friend had pleaded tiredness last night — she didn't want to give Grace a chance to talk or ask questions. Had Sequoyah slept at all, or had she only feigned slumber until she was sure Grace was sleeping?

Reaching the *kuugh'a*, Grace slung her saddlebag over her shoulder and exchanged her moccasins for boots.

Then she grabbed Joe's belongings from his wickiup and raced back to find the horses ready to go. She swung up into the saddle beside him.

"Which way do you think they went?" she asked.

Joe pointed to the trail toward town. "Looks like fresh hoofprints and some horse droppings over there, but I doubt they'll stick to the trail for long. They'd know better. We'll need to watch for signs of where they veered off."

Grace nodded. As they followed the prints in the soft earth, she searched for broken twigs or disturbed dirt in the undergrowth. Beside her, Joe sat alert and tense, his eyes scanning for clues. The trail narrowed until they could no longer ride side by side, and Joe took the lead. Bullet chafed at the slow pace, but they couldn't take a chance of missing any signs of which way their friends had gone — Dahana was an excellent tracker. He'd know to cover their movements, even if they didn't expect anyone to be trailing them.

"They couldn't have gotten far, could they?" Grace asked.

Joe shrugged. "Any idea how long they've been gone?"

"Sequoyah rolled over and went to sleep a few minutes after we settled for the night. At least I *thought* she was sleeping . . ."

"So she could have left any time after you fell asleep."

"Yes." Grace tried to recall the evening before. "I was pretty tired, but I did lie there for a while, thinking . . ."

She bit her lip as memories of last night returned. Pictures of her and Joe entwined in each other's arms. She'd relived every moment of their evening together, each time with a different ending. In the end, in her mind, she'd drifted off to sleep safe in Joe's arms.

"Oh?" His voice interrupted her reverie.

"Umm, yeah. I was probably awake for a little while." Grace was glad Joe was riding in front so he couldn't see her flaming cheeks. "I was just . . . glad to be back. I loved listening to the quiet, hearing the night sounds." Her words sounded pathetic even to herself.

Joe chuckled. "I tossed and turned most of the night too." He glanced over his shoulder with a warm gaze. "Thinking of you."

So she wasn't the only one. "Me too," Grace admitted, her memory of Joe's heartbeat close to hers and his lips on hers still crowding her mind. She was so lost in thought, she didn't realize Joe was still staring at her. Her face grew even hotter.

"So," he said softly, "I spent the night with you in my dreams. Where did you spend yours?"

Grace cleared her throat. "Joe, we need to pay attention to the trail . . ."

Joe looked embarrassed. "You're right. That's what you do to me, Grace. You make me forget everything else," he said with a smile.

She swallowed. No one had ever made her feel this

special before, and in a way that's what made Joe so dangerous. Being around him made her forget too — and if she stayed at the camp too long, she might give up her mission completely. Only the thought of avenging Abby, who never had a chance to grow up, kept her going. And young Emily, who *would* get that chance, as long as Grace kept her safe until she and Caroline got on that train. But what of the other young girls and their families whom the gang might kill? The only way to protect them was to see every member of the Guiltless Gang behind bars.

Bullet stopped abruptly, and she looked up to see that Joe had reined in Paint. "What is it?"

Joe pointed to some broken branches to the right. A narrow trail snaked through the trees at a steep angle. "Think they went that way?"

Tree branches drooped so low and tangled overhead, Sequoyah and Dahana would have had to get off and lead the horses.

Joe dismounted. "Why don't you wait here a second? I'll check out the trail to see if they left any clues." He handed Grace Paint's reins. "Be right back."

Grace wanted to go with him, to use her own tracking skills, but it was probably best he went alone. Her mind was churning with so many conflicting feelings, she wasn't sure she could concentrate. She smiled a little, remembering Joe's response back in the saloon when she told him he was a distraction — his fingertips running up the back of her hand . . . She sighed, exasperated at herself. It seemed she couldn't even keep her mind on simple tasks when he was around. She was sure she'd made the right choice when she rode away alone from the Ndeh village, but just thinking about it made Grace's heart ache. The more time she spent around Joe, the harder it was to go on without him. Maybe what she had to do was focus on how she could stick to her task *and* keep him in her life. They'd just have to set up some limits, some ground rules, like they had discussed the night before . . .

Joe thrashed back up the hill toward her, breaking her thoughts. "I'm not sure, but it looks as if someone leading horses went this way recently."

"Then let's follow that trail." Grace slid off Bullet and handed Paint's reins to Joe. This time she took the lead. Looking for clues would keep her mind from straying to thoughts of Joe, and the trail was too narrow to walk beside each other, so Grace forced herself to forget his presence and watch for signs of Sequoyah and Dahana.

They walked for a good few hours on the windy, twisty, narrow trail, but the only clues they'd seen were some recent horse droppings, and they had no way to tell for certain if they were from Sequoyah's and Dahana's horses. Branches scratched Grace's face, and the sun blazed hot, causing sweat to trickle down her neck despite the protection of her hat's brim.

Joe stopped a moment to wipe his face. "We need water

and so do the horses. Let's take a break," he said, motioning to a nearby rock.

Grace sank onto the rock beside him, but then wriggled away so they weren't touching.

"Afraid of me?" Joe asked with a half-smile.

"We need to concentrate on finding Sequoyah," Grace said firmly. If she let herself get drawn in, she'd find herself in Joe's arms in no time.

He grinned more widely. "So you plan to stay a safe distance from me?" He paused. "It might be wise. Especially if you knew all the thoughts running through my head . . ."

Grace swallowed and shuffled even farther away. Joe chuckled.

"Relax. I won't try to take advantage of you." He sobered. "I'm as worried about finding Sequoyah and Dahana as you are. I can't believe they'd run off like this. If they've eloped, there's no hope her father will forgive her. They won't be welcome with their people anymore."

Grace ached inside for her friend. "Why would she do this? She knows the consequences."

"People do strange things for love."

Joe's wistful tone touched Grace's heart. She understood how love could make you lose all track of time, all sense of purpose, all connection with the outside world. It blocked everything but thoughts of the other person. But to sacrifice their whole future?

Grace sympathized with Sequoyah, though — marrying Tarak would turn her stomach too. She couldn't forget the way he'd mocked her and Joe, and his rage when Joe taught her the Ndeh ways. The ugliness in his eyes, the cruel barbs and taunts he'd thrown at her? No, Sequoyah was right to avoid living with such a man.

Grace turned to Joe. "She turned Tarak down publicly. Why didn't she tell Cheis then how she felt about Dahana? Her father is a fair man."

She thought about how Cheis had forgiven her, Grace, for breaking a taboo when she'd killed that javelina and dragged it back to camp. Even now she cringed when she remembered the shock on everyone's faces, and the horror in Joe's eyes as he hurried her away to explain that to kill and eat certain animals was forbidden for the Ndeh; her triumph had quickly turned to shame. She'd wanted to run away and hide, but Cheis had understood her brave intentions. He presented her with the quiver and arrows she kept slung over her shoulders to this day. He'd made the gift into an offering of forgiveness and shown her through his deeds that it was better to forgive and love another. Surely he would be as generous with his own daughter?

"Joe?" Grace looked over to find him staring at her with a look that made her insides feel fluttery. "Cheis will forgive Sequoyah, won't he? Remember the javelina? He forgave me after I'd done something forbidden."

Joe looked grave. "This is different. You were an outsider and didn't know their traditions. Sequoyah's a chief's daughter. Her actions will shame him. People will no longer look to him as a leader if he cannot control his own family."

"That's so sad," Grace burst out. "What about Sequoyah? She loves Dahana. It seems so unfair. And how will they live if they're cast out of the camp?"

"That's what worries me most," Joe replied. "With the soldiers on the lookout for renegades, two Ndeh alone will be an easy target. And if Sequoyah makes the foolish mistake of going into town again for supplies, she'll be risking her life."

"Do you really think it was her?" Grace had a hard time picturing Sequoyah doing anything that reckless.

"Where else would they get the supplies to elope?"

He was right. As much as she wanted to think of Sequoyah as sensible, running off to marry was impetuous and dangerous. Her fear for her friends grew, settling uneasily in her stomach.

Joe stood and dusted himself off. "We'd better get going. No telling how much of a head start they had, or even if this is the trail they followed."

Grace jumped to her feet. "We can't let them make a mistake that they can never undo." She snatched Bullet's reins and pressed on, ignoring the fierce midday sun.

When the trail moved steeply downhill again, Joe

insisted on going first. Heavy sticks in hand to prevent falling and as a defense against snakes, they descended through the undergrowth, following tiny signs of broken branches, light hoofprints, and occasional horse manure. They emerged from the trees into a rocky area of boulders and sparse vegetation. High mounds of hoodoos rose on both sides — tall, thin spires of multi-colored rock throwing tiny patches of shade across the path. Granite outcroppings blocked their view of the canyon below, but they could ride the horses again, side by side. They mounted and, watching for gravel slides and teetering boulders, picked their way along the ridge on a trail that wound up and down the steep inclines.

By now the sun was almost directly overhead. It scorched them, and sweat poured from Grace's brow. When they reached a flat grassy area, she reined Bullet to a halt.

"We have to give the horses another quick rest," she said. After dismounting, they watered the horses and Grace let Bullet nibble some grass. Around them upright spikes of blooming agave and creosote bushes heavy with yellow flowers dotted the landscape. Some of the agave stalks towered overhead, heavy with greenish-yellow flower clusters. If she had more time, she would have harvested some of these plants for Cheveyo, the Ndeh shaman. Before she'd left the camp on her mission, Cheveyo had been teaching her and Sequoyah to make herbal remedies.

Maybe someday soon she and Sequoyah could come back and gather these — but first she and Joe had to find her. Joe set Paint free and flopped onto the hard ground between two gigantic boulders, and Grace slumped down beside him. She slid lower until the large mass of stone in front of her blocked the sun and shaded her face, fanning herself with her hat and glancing back up at the trail they'd traversed. By now the Ndeh would be busy with their usual daily tasks, and Sequoyah and Dahana's absence would be obvious. She turned to Joe.

"Everyone must know Sequoyah's gone. Some people may think Dahana went out hunting alone but most will guess the truth."

"They will," Joe said. "Dahana prefers to hunt with groups. They'd think it odd that he went out alone."

"We're probably too late to save their reputations . . ."

Joe nodded. "I thought we'd have caught up with them by now, but if they left soon after you fell asleep we may not find them at all. They could be hours ahead of us."

"We don't even know for sure they came this way," Grace said dejectedly, sipping her water slowly and then stashing the pouch in her saddlebag. She stretched her aching muscles. Traveling this rough terrain was hard on them and on the horses, but if they had any chance of catching Sequoyah they needed to keep moving. "I hope we're not following someone else's tracks."

"Most likely it's them. No one else would take such a

circuitous route when they could travel the normal path down the trail. If we just knew where they were headed, we could cut hours from this trip."

When Joe whistled for Paint, Bullet pricked up his ears, trotting after his fellow horse and standing patiently while Grace remounted. She patted her palomino's neck. "You've been so good, Bullet. I know this isn't easy."

"And so have you." Joe smiled innocently at Grace. "This is rough terrain, but you've managed to keep up."

"Oh, you . . . you . . ." Grace shook a fist at Joe playfully. "I grew up on horseback, I'll have you know."

Joe thrust out his lower lip as if his feelings were hurt. "I was hoping you'd mention again what a wonderful teacher you had. You know, the one who taught you to track like this?"

Grace wrinkled her nose. "Oh, him." She waved her hand airily. "I only pretended to need help so I could spend time with him."

"Oh, really? You found me that irresistible?"

"I wouldn't say that."

"What would you say?"

Good question. Originally, all she'd wanted was training so she could get revenge on her family's killers, but she had to admit spending time alone with Joe had soon become equally compelling.

He turned mock-sad eyes at her. "If it's taking you this long, maybe I don't want to hear the answer . . ."

Grace moved Bullet close enough to Paint that she could teasingly swat Joe's arm. "You know how I feel about you."

"But it never hurts to hear it." Joe's gaze turned from teasing to soft and serious. "And you know how I feel about you."

Grace's heart thumped so hard she was sure Joe could hear it over the horse's hooves. She clucked to Bullet and pulled ahead to break eye contact. At first, all those months ago, she admired him from afar but convinced herself that the tingling his touch evoked was only because she wasn't used to being around men. But now those feelings had grown into an overwhelming desire that threatened to engulf her.

By mid-afternoon the skies had grown cloudy. Lightning flashed across the sky, and booms followed soon after, and they knew heat lightning could soon turn into a sudden deluge. Afternoon thunderstorms were common this time of year, and water often gushed down the mountains, overflowing the arroyos. If that happened now, the water would wash out the trail they were following. Grace's heart sank.

Joe cast a wary glance overhead. "We need to find shelter." He pointed to a ledge below with a rocky outcropping above it. "Head for that overhang," he said, riding past Grace. "I'll look for a safe place for us to wait out the storm."

Grace struggled to control Bullet, who shied at each crash of thunder. She urged him after Paint. A short while later, Joe waved to her from under the outcropping.

"Over here! There's a small cave we can both fit inside."

Bullet twitched with another explosion of thunder, his body tensed, and he grew skittish. Grace headed Bullet anxiously toward the spot where Joe was waiting, but a sudden flash was followed by a boom so close she jumped. Another flash lit the trail right in front of her, and she cried out in surprise as up above them, a huge oak split in two. Half of it crashed down in front of her, blocking her path, and Bullet neighed and shied away, dancing backward. To her horror, the falling tree set off an avalanche. Boulders tumbled down the hill, gravel rained down around her. Bullet reared and twisted out of the way as a boulder plunged toward them.

"Grace!"

Joe's scream came to her over the rising winds and the rumbles of thunder. Again and again he called her name, but he couldn't see anything past the tree. Grace's throat had closed in fear — when she tried to reply, her answer was so raspy it was lost in the wind. She was shaking so hard she could hardly hold the reins. If Bullet hadn't been so wary, they both would have been crushed.

She tamped down her nerves and struggled to answer Joe's frantic cries. "I'm fine," she yelled, but her words were drowned in a blast of thunder that echoed through the nearby canyon. The tree blocked the only access to the ledge where Joe had taken shelter. The pile of boulders cut off her descent down the mountain. She and Bullet were trapped.

And overhead, a rock teetered precariously.

CHAPTER 17

A jolt of lightning lit the nearby sky, and thunder shook the ground under Grace's feet. The rock overhead wobbled dangerously. Keeping an eye on it, she eased Bullet backward slowly and up the trail out of harm's way, but the lightning presented an even graver threat.

Pa had taught her to stay low during the rare lightning storms in the desert and to seek shelter immediately. Talking calmly to Bullet, Grace slid off the horse's back. She could crouch, but Bullet needed to be protected. Frantically, she searched for refuge. Trees and boulders were too hazardous, but staying in the open was even more dangerous. If only she could get to Joe.

She stood, pressing against Bullet's quivering side and

stroking his neck, talking soothingly to him. She kept a tight grip on the reins, hoping to keep him from bolting. Joe's cries had become desperate, but they sounded closer. If only she could see past the tree and rocks, she could signal to him that they were safe.

"Joe," she screamed, "we're fine. Stay safe."

Lightning crackled so close that the hairs on the back of Grace's neck lifted. Her face and palms tingled, and Bullet trembled. The thunderclap that followed deafened her. When she could hear again, a sound of thrashing in the nearby fallen tree made her heart race. Had an animal been trapped? By the sound of it, it was huge. Grace shivered and stepped back. Mountain lions ranged through this area. They usually hunted at night, although they often could be spotted at dusk or dawn. But if the falling tree or boulders had disturbed one's den . . .

Bullet tossed his head and widened his nostrils. He'd saved her from a bear attack once, but almost lost his life in the process. She couldn't let that happen again. Grace whipped out her gun.

Keeping her eye trained on the movement of the lower branches, she aimed. Tawny color rippled in the greenery, edging closer. Its movements were too uneven, too frantic for her to get a clear shot. She hated to kill it, but she didn't trust an enraged mountain lion or any wild animal not to pounce, especially if its home had been destroyed. With a loud crack, the branches broke and something shot into the clearing. Grace's scream died in her throat as the blur turned into Joe, his hair tousled, his face scratched and bleeding. Hands shaking, she lowered the gun. She'd almost shot him. Tremors coursed through her at the thought, and she could barely slide the gun back in its holster.

"Grace!" Joe shouted. He raced toward her, caught her in his arms, and whirled her around. "You're safe. You're safe." He stepped back to look at her. "I thought the tree crushed you. I thought you were —" His voice was as shaky as her body. "When I didn't hear you answer . . ." He shuddered.

Lightning flashed directly overhead. Joe tackled her, throwing his body over hers. When the thunder echoed from the sky, he jumped to his feet and held out his hand. "We have to get to safety." He dragged her toward the tree. "You can crawl through the opening I made."

"I can't leave Bullet."

"Grace, it's you I care about." Joe glanced around. "I don't see any way to get him through."

"I won't go without him," she said, stubbornly planting her feet.

Joe motioned toward the tree. "Fine, you head toward Paint. I'll stay with Bullet."

Her eyes widened with worry. "He's my horse."

"Grace, just go." Joe's voice was filled with anguish. "I've spent years in these mountains. I can get Bullet to safety much faster than you can." He took her by the shoulders and pushed her toward the opening.

Grace struggled to free herself from his grip.

"You don't have to do everything alone. Please," Joe begged. "Let me do this for you." He whirled her around and kissed her briefly on the lips. "Just trust me."

They crouched beside the tree as another flash lit up the sky. The boom shook Grace's chest and almost knocked her from her feet.

"Now, Grace. I promise to get Bullet through this."

Much as she hated to admit it, Joe was right. She couldn't put Bullet in more danger because of her inexperience with this terrain. She ducked low and crept through the broken branches. Her hat tumbled off to hang by its wind string around her neck. Twigs poked at her eyes, gouging her cheek, snagging hair from her braid. When she emerged on the other side, she stayed in a crouch and ran toward the ledge where Paint stood. Heart thumping, she ducked into the cave and sat near the entrance watching for Joe. If anything happened to him, she'd never forgive herself.

The cave was too low to see past the fallen tree and rockslide. She drew up her knees, wrapped her arms around them, and stared off toward the hill, willing Joe and Bullet to appear. Finally, she saw a moving speck in the distance — high up, above the fallen rocks. She followed the movement but couldn't tell for sure if it was them.

The spot picked its way across the rough terrain, at times stopping, then starting again. When they drew close enough for her to make out that it was a man and a horse, she chanted "be safe" with each step they took, and she cringed at every lightning strike. Bullet seemed to be cooperating. Joe had learned the Ndeh way of gentling horses, and even when the flashes of light made Bullet threaten to bolt — and Grace's heart rise in her throat — he managed to keep hold of the horse. When they finally made it to the ledge, Grace wanted to jump up and hug Joe tightly, but even after all the danger, she remembered her intention to keep her hands to herself. Joe settled Bullet and then ducked into the cave, and she smiled at him.

"Thank you for taking care of him. I'm so glad you both made it safely."

Joe gave her a tender glance. "And I'm glad you're safe. Thank you for trusting me."

Grace only nodded, her heart too full of gratitude to express it in words.

As the storm's fury increased, the lightning moved uphill. Dark clouds followed, unleashing torrents of rain.

"Oh, no." Joe sucked in a breath. "That rain water will come crashing down through the arroyos soon. I hope Sequoyah and Dahana are all right."

Grace had been so worried about the weather, she'd forgotten her friend. "They know to take shelter. Even I learned that in the short time I was with the Ndeh."

"I'm more concerned about whether they're in a place where they *can* be protected. If they're out of the mountains and in the desert . . ."

She swallowed. "Let's hope they found somewhere safe."

Joe nodded. A short while later, with a loud roar, water gushed down the mountain, cutting through the well-worn channel of an arroyo. The winding slash deep in the mountainside turned from tan, baked, and cracking ground to a tumbling, swirling black fury, sweeping away everything in its path.

CHAPTER 18

Joe slid closer to Grace and put his arm around her. In spite of herself, she laid her head on his shoulder — after everything that had happened, she welcomed his comfort. Together they watched the storm until it died out. As quickly as it had begun, the rain stopped, but water still cascaded past like white-water rapids overflowing the riverbanks.

As soon as the lightning had stopped, Joe scooted from the cave and stood looking down. "We're not far from level ground, but the water will have washed away all traces of their tracks. I have no idea how we'll find them from here."

"Maybe we should think about where they might be heading. Would they go into town?"

Joe studied the mountains above them, then traced their path with his finger. "We started there, followed that ridgeline, wound back along that mountain trail, then switched directions and moved down toward the canyon."

Their route resembled the snaky curves of a sidewinder's body. Grace gestured behind them toward town. "So they're not headed to Bisbee or Tombstone. What's the nearest town in that direction?"

Joe shrugged. "I normally head toward Tombstone. I've never explored much in this direction, but the train heads out this way."

"There's sure to be a large town somewhere along here if we follow the railroad tracks."

They picked their way carefully down through the rocky ground, avoiding the rushing water. When they got to flat ground, they searched the horizon in both directions. The road back to town appeared deserted, but in the distance, heading in the opposite direction, two riders walked their horses beside the railway tracks.

Grace squinted, but the figures were blurry. In spite of that, her spirits rose finally. "Joe, look! That must be them. Hurry!"

Joe took off at a gallop and she raced after him. As she drew closer, he urged Paint faster. Her braid streaming behind her, hat bouncing on her back, Grace passed him, letting the wind carry away all her sorrows as they flew along. She leaned into the sheer joy of riding and became one with Bullet.

They were almost upon the other couple when the woman turned. It *was* Sequoyah! Grace rushed toward her, calling her friend's name. Sequoyah's eyebrows raised in surprise, and then a troubled look crossed her face. She and Dahana stopped and turned, and Grace and Joe slowed, panting from exertion but smiling in relief. She had won that riding competition, and she let Joe know it by whooping and shaking a fist over her head.

He pretended to frown, but when their gazes met his face grew tender, and he smiled indulgently. "I let you win," he said in a teasing voice.

Grace acted indignant. "You did not. I beat you, fair and square."

"You never play fair, Grace Milton." A deeper meaning lay behind those words, and he cocked his head to one side and studied her intently.

A movement from Sequoyah drew their attention. She sat astride her horse, arms crossed, an annoyed frown on her face. "What you doing here?"

"We came to take you back home." She hoped Sequoyah would cooperate, especially after all they'd been through to find them. "Before you do something you regret."

"Please. Don't be foolish," Joe begged.

"Love is not foolish." Sequoyah motioned toward both of them, but her gaze was fixed on Grace. "You know this.

You love him." She rounded on Joe. "And you. You do this" — she mimicked a hangdog expression and downcast eyes — "when Grace go away."

Joe looked sheepish. "I missed her, that's true. And we both understand that you want to be together, but —"

"But it is not wise," Grace finished. "Why not tell your father of your love? Ask if he will let you be together?"

Sequoyah's jaw hardened and she shook her head. "He not understand. He want me to marry Tarak." Her eyes burned with fury. "I not want that."

"I can understand why," Grace said quickly, but Joe gave her a warning frown.

"We belong together." Sequoyah gestured to her own heart and then to Dahana's.

Dahana broke in and spoke sharply and rapidly in their own language. His words flew out of his mouth so quickly that Grace could understand only a few of them. She frowned in concentration, but gave up as his voice rose and he gestured, throwing his arms out wide. Joe interrupted and spoke in slow, measured tones. The unfamiliar words sounded soothing, conciliatory.

Dahana's angry posture relaxed a bit but the stubborn tilt of his chin remained.

Joe held out a pleading hand and Grace recognized the words "please," "father," "love," and "help," but she could follow no more of the conversation. She assumed that Joe was offering to help them, and a softness came over

Sequoyah's face as he continued his plea. She looked at Dahana with a question in her eyes.

Grace waited until Joe was done speaking, then she added a plea of her own, hoping it reinforced what Joe had said. "Please come back with us. We'll talk to your father, get him to see that you and Dahana love each other and should be together."

Joe's gentle smile told her she had said the right thing. Dahana's rapid-fire response was a cross between anger and fear, and Grace wished she knew what they were saying so she could support Joe's appeal.

She said the only thing she could. "Please?" She held out a hand to Sequoyah. The hand of friendship, understanding, and acceptance.

Sequoyah stared at the outstretched hand, then at Grace's face and nodded ever so slightly. She turned to Dahana and said a couple more soft words, and his back stiffened. He turned away for a moment, but after Sequoyah added a few gentle words, he addressed Joe. His face was tight and his words pinged like bullets. Then Dahana turned his horse away from them a short distance, and Sequoyah followed. They bent their heads together and spoke rapidly, punctuated with many hand gestures.

Grace turned questioning eyes to Joe. "What were you saying?"

"I think I convinced them to come back. At least,

Sequoyah wants to return. Dahana is reluctant. He's more afraid of the punishment that awaits her — he doesn't want to see her rejected by her family and by the whole band. What you said helped. I know Sequoyah trusts you."

"So they're discussing it?"

Joe nodded. "I think she'll prevail. A man will do anything the woman he loves asks."

"Oh, really," Grace said, a glint in her eye, but genuine hope in her heart. "He'd even agree that she should chase down the Guiltless Gang?"

The look of admiration in Joe's eyes changed to reluctance. "He wouldn't want to see her in danger — ever — but . . ."

He didn't get to finish the sentence because Dahana wheeled his horse and headed back toward them, his face set in a stony expression.

Sequoyah followed more slowly, teary-eyed. She gave Grace a tremulous smile. "We go back. I tell Dahana you help. He not want to but . . ."

What Joe said was true. Sequoyah looked relieved, but it was tempered by fear.

"Grace, you tell my father to let us marry? He listen to you."

Grace's stomach twisted. What if she couldn't convince Cheis? Who was she to interfere in a family relationship? She didn't even know the Ndeh customs. She looked to Joe for reassurance and his beaming smile gave her confidence.

If he thought she could do it, she would. Somehow she had to find a way to make Cheis see that Sequoyah and Dahana belonged together.

They turned all their horses and set off for the village. Grace and Sequoyah took the lead, but they'd gone only a few steps when a loud roar sounded overhead.

"Watch out!" Joe screamed.

Grace wheeled Bullet in the nick of time, but Sequoyah wasn't so lucky. Storm water plunged suddenly down the mountain, raging straight toward them.

CHAPTER 19

The force of the water knocked Sequoyah's horse off balance, and before the pinto could regain his footing, Sequoyah tumbled into the water. The current dragged her along, tossing her as she flailed her arms and tried to stay afloat. Farther upstream the pinto swam for shore.

Grace had no time to think. Acting on instinct, she galloped past the spot where Sequoyah was floundering. She had to make it downstream to rescue her. Eyes on her friend, she failed to see the obstacle in their path. She pitched forward as Bullet launched into the air, grasping desperately onto his mane and only just managing to hang on as the horse leaped over it. Below them, a huge lumpy mound of sand covered the ground. Something glittered at the edge but Grace had no time to identify it. She checked to make sure no more obstacles blocked their path, then turned her attention back to the struggling Sequoyah.

Racing a good distance downstream, Grace dismounted and tied a rope quickly around Bullet's saddle horn. After securing it to her waist, she waded into the fiercely swirling waters, her heart pounding desperately. The churning current almost swept her off her feet.

Behind her, Joe shouted, "Grace, don't! You'll get washed away."

He and Dahana galloped toward her but she kept her eyes on Sequoyah's bobbing head. A sudden rush of water knocked her off her feet, and she fought to get her footing, clinging to the rope as it burned her palms, storm water filling her mouth. She finally clawed her way to the surface, moving determinedly out toward Sequoyah, panic rising each time her friend's head disappeared under the water. When Sequoyah tumbled near enough, Grace lunged.

"Hold on to the rope," she shouted as she dragged Sequoyah toward her.

The current pummeled them, driving them farther downstream, and water smacked their faces, but Grace clutched at Sequoyah's arm firmly. They struggled to the surface, fighting the current that tried to tear them apart, but she managed to place the rope in Sequoyah's hands. Once she had a firm hold, Grace called out to Bullet.

By then, Joe and Dahana had dismounted, and Joe eased the horse back in slow increments, towing them toward dry land.

When they reached dry ground, the two of them lay panting and gasping for breath. Grace felt her arms begin to shake with the struggle to keep hold of the rope, and her clothes were heavy with water.

"Thank you . . ." Sequoyah gasped out. "Oh, thank you. Oh, Grace. You . . . are . . . like . . . Lozen," she managed to splutter, then she rolled onto her side and retched out more rainwater.

"Lozen," Dahana said with a nod, squatting beside Sequoyah and patting her back.

Grace turned to Joe. "Who's Lozen?"

His eyes shone with admiration. "She's a great Ndeh heroine. When the Ndeh were fleeing the cavalry, they reached the banks of the Rio Grande. The men turned to fight, but Lozen wanted to protect the women and children — they had to get to the other side of the river, where they would be safe, but the river raged so hard, they were afraid. Rifle held aloft, she plunged into the waters. Her horse swam across, and when they saw she could do it, the others followed. Once she had gotten everyone to safety, she rushed back across the river to join the warriors."

Grace smiled. "She sounds like a remarkable woman." She could understand Lozen's drive to protect those she loved.

Still choking, Sequoyah pushed herself up on one elbow, struggling to sit up. "We go now."

Dahana helped her to her feet and onto her horse. He tried to insist on her riding with him, but Sequoyah refused.

"Hang on. I need to check something before we go," Grace called over her shoulder. She headed toward the mound Bullet had jumped. It seemed so odd and out of place in the flat landscape, she had to see what it was that had sent her flying. Beneath a small group of mesquite trees, she found it. Storm waters had dislodged the handle of a shovel. The scrap of heavy canvas covering it flapped in the swirling torrent, and she lifted the edge of the soggy material. Layers of sand and dirt had been piled over the fabric to hide whatever was beneath. Using all her strength, she tugged it back to find more tools, logs, old railway ties, and several cylinders with string dangling from one end. Grace had just picked up one to examine it when Joe came over.

"Don't touch that!" His voice rang out, sharp and alarmed.

Grace dropped it and turned. "Why?"

"It's dynamite."

Although she'd heard of miners using dynamite, she'd never seen any. Why would a miner bury supplies way out here, miles from the mountains? She looked up at Joe about to ask that very question when her gaze lit on the railway tracks. Almost breathless, she asked, "Is it for a train robbery?"

Joe squatted beside her. "Hmm . . . logs to block the tracks, dynamite to break open the safe carrying the gold. Could be."

Grace's heartbeat quickened. "Well, what should we do with it?"

Dahana and Sequoyah came over quickly. Sequoyah was shivering and her teeth were chattering. Grace couldn't ask her friends to wait. Quickly, she re-covered the spot and made a mental note of where the stash was located so she could come back later. Was this connected to the Andersens asking about train tickets? If this stash belonged to the Andersen twins, they could be preparing to stage a holdup . . .

* * *

Dripping wet and bedraggled, the four of them began the trek up the mountain, this time on a well-used trail that was a direct route instead of the circuitous path they'd taken down. Without traversing the many ridges and backtracking, they reached the Ndeh camp within a couple of hours.

Cheis strode toward them, his features contorted in rage. He ignored his daughter and spoke to Joe, his words laced with anger. Again, Grace struggled to understand. Joe dismounted, crossed his arms, and shook his head.

At his firm response and unyielding stance, surprise crossed Cheis's face. Then his jaw tightened and he spat out a few words.

"What's he saying?" Grace hissed, but Joe motioned her to silence.

Beside her, Sequoyah hung her head. "He say I shame my family." The sorrow in her eyes made Grace's heart ache for her.

She leaned over and whispered, "Does he understand you love Dahana?"

"Joe not say that. He listen. My father say Tarak is a good man. Good hunter." With each word, hope leaked from Sequoyah's face and her tone reflected her discouragement. Tears sprang to her eyes as Cheis turned and started to march away.

"Wait," Grace cried. She had no idea what had been said, but she couldn't watch Sequoyah's dreams slip away or see her be alienated from her family. With no idea of proper protocol, she slid from Bullet's back and ran after Cheis. "Please, let me talk to you."

The chief stopped, but he remained with his back toward his daughter, a symbol of his rejection. Grace walked around to face him, her hands outstretched in pleading. Her words tumbled out. "You can't turn your back on Sequoyah. She loves you. You're a family." Seeing Cheis's frown, she stopped. Had she said something taboo?

"I not understand you."

Grace had been talking rapidly, and Cheis struggled with English, but the stiffness of his posture and the rigidness of his face also indicated that he had no desire to hear her words. She didn't let that stop her. Sequoyah's future was at stake. She repeated her words slowly, then continued, "I do not know your customs." She bowed her head slightly, hoping it would be understood as a gesture of humility. "But I know that families belong together." She swallowed back tears at the thought of her own family.

A flicker of compassion crossed Cheis's face but it was quickly replaced by sternness. He hadn't stalked off, so Grace continued, word by slow word. She pleaded Sequoyah and Dahana's case, describing their love for each other, and added an appeal for Cheis to allow the couple to marry.

He interrupted, his words hard and clipped. "Tarak is good hunter. He care for her. Dahana —" His dismissive hand gesture indicated that he thought the young brave an inferior choice.

Aside from Joe, Tarak was the best hunter in the Ndeh band. Though it pained Grace to say it about the man who considered her an enemy, she had to let Cheis know she understood his view. "Tarak is" — she choked out the words — "an excellent hunter, yes. He would be a wonderful provider."

Cheis crossed his arms and rocked back on his heels. He looked slightly pacified.

"But as a father, you want only the best for your daughter."

"This is true," Cheis agreed.

Before Cheis could add that Tarak was the best choice, Grace hurried on. "Dahana may not be the best hunter . . ." She sent an apologetic glance his way, but judging from the way his brows were drawn together in concentration, Dahana was having trouble following the conversation. Cheis grunted in agreement.

"But he has something Tarak lacks."

Seeing a look of incomprehension in Cheis's eyes, Grace simplified her words. "Dahana *loves* Sequoyah. He will care for her well. He will do his very best." She took a chance. "Do you want your daughter to be happy?"

Cheis waved away her question. "She be happy with good hunter. Have full belly."

Grace nodded. "Yes, she needs to eat. But she also wants to be with the man she loves."

"She learn to love Tarak."

Grace drew in a frustrated breath. How could she make him understand? But before she could speak again, a hand settled on her shoulder. Joe stood beside her. He looked Cheis in the eye. "What Grace says is true." He launched into a rapid speech that she did not understand, and a far-away look of sadness entered Cheis's eyes. He stared down at the ground, his head bowed. When he responded to Joe's apparent question, his voice was husky.

Grace longed to know what was being said, but she was reluctant to interrupt when Joe's words seemed to be having such an effect. She stood silently, willing Joe to say the right words, the words that would touch Cheis's heart.

A long pause followed Joe's speech.

At last, Cheis responded in English. "I cannot." He moved to step around them and his bent back spoke of his sorrow. Joe tried once more, but the chief snapped out an answer. Grace glanced up, hoping for a translation, and Joe whispered the sentence.

"To elope is taboo."

The weight of Cheis's words hung in the air.

Many of the people who had gathered now turned to go, but Grace could not let the matter rest. "You would let this rule come between you and your daughter?"

Cheis gave her a look of pity, as if she were too young and naive to understand. "It is our way."

"No. Forgiveness is your way." Grace toned down the shrillness in her voice and continued more softly. "Forgiveness is what you taught me, what you showed me. I broke a taboo, and you forgave me."

"You did not know."

She sighed. "Do you love your daughter?"

"I love her much."

"Then show Sequoyah that by forgiving her."

He was quiet for a painfully long time before he finally spoke. "I will think on your words."

Cheis walked toward his *kuugh'a* heavily and slowly, his shoulders bowed.

Grace had no idea what his decision would be.

CHAPTER 20

The next morning, Cheis emerged from his wickiup with a grave look on his face and called a council meeting of the elders. As usual, Joe joined them. Grace stayed with Sequoyah, who was half-heartedly picking medicinal herbs while throwing nervous glances over her shoulder at the meeting place. Dahana was keeping his distance. Grace was worried about what would happen if Cheis did not unbend his stance. Would Sequoyah and Dahana be told to leave?

She remembered one incident that happened while she was living with the Ndeh: after several warnings, a man who hadn't cared properly for his ageing parents had been cast out of the band. She'd heard that many who were forced out of the group did not survive, and Grace's stomach knotted at the thought of her friends being shunned like that. Perhaps she and Joe had done more harm than good.

As time passed, Sequoyah gave up any pretense of work and sat back on her heels, staring off into the distance. Grace's heart ached for her, desperate to know what the Cheis's decision was. Finally, a short while later, Joe exited the meeting tent and headed their way, his expression inscrutable. At Grace's questioning look, he only shook his head.

"I've come to get Sequoyah and Dahana."

At the sound of her name, Sequoyah jumped up, upsetting her basket. She looked ready to cry when she saw the scattered herbs. After Grace reassured her that she'd pick them up, Sequoyah stood wringing her hands. She waited until Dahana appeared with Joe, and then the three of them headed off together. Grace watched as they disappeared inside the *kuugh'a*, then worked rapidly to keep her mind off her worries. But fears about the stash she'd uncovered near the train tracks also intruded on her concern for Sequoyah. Was it the Andersens? It seemed so likely that it would be, but how soon would they strike? And which train?

Grace was so caught up in her apprehension she almost missed Sequoyah and Dahana leaving the council meeting — but she was thrilled when she saw Sequoyah's glowing face and Dahana's broad smile.

Sequoyah raced over and took Grace's hands. "He say we can be together!"

Dahana added in halting English, "Thank you, Grace."

"Oh, I'm so happy for you both!" With a quick hug for her friend, Grace wished them both the very best. Looking from Sequoyah's beaming expression to Dahana's, she knew they had a wonderful future ahead. She noticed that Tarak was nowhere to be seen around the camp — she wondered how he would react to the news . . .

Grace felt her muscles relax as she realized that things were going to be all right for her friends at the camp. Now she had to get back to town and find out as much as she could about the Andersens and the possible train robbery. She couldn't risk losing this lead. She looked for Joe but couldn't find him, and she assumed he was still with the elders. In the meantime, she decided to go prepare Bullet. Hurrying over to the enclosure, she whistled and waited for Bullet to charge across the ground to where she was standing, but then jumped as Joe came up behind her.

"Did you plan to leave without me?" His tone was light, but there was worry in his eyes.

"I have to get back to town. If the Andersen twins have a train robbery planned, I need to stop them."

"Grace?" Joe turned her to face him. "This sheriff isn't like Behan. Give him a chance. Talk to him."

She turned away. "I already have, and I ended up having to catch Plimpton on my own."

"This is a potential train robbery. He'll take it seriously, I'm sure of it." Joe began to saddle up Paint as Grace readied Bullet, and she raised an eyebrow at him. "I'm coming with you," he said with an air of finality.

Grace wanted to say she didn't need his help, that he would only be a distraction, but having company on the ride back to town would be nice, and she might need backup — something she couldn't count on from the sheriff. She remembered her hope to stick to her mission as well as finding a way to be with him too . . .

She was wondering if she might regret her decision, though, when the whole way to town Joe pestered her about talking to the sheriff, until she finally caved in and agreed. When they arrived, Grace tried to put it off by saying she had to hire somewhere to sleep that night, but Joe accompanied her to the saloon while she asked Miz Bessie for two nights in the attic room.

The saloonkeeper looked a bit miffed. "Think you can waltz in here anytime and that room'll be waiting for you?"

Grace's heart sank. "It's not available?" She started to put her money back in her reticule.

"It's available," Miz Bessie said grudgingly, holding out her hand.

After she paid, Joe pulled out a small pouch of gold. "I'd also like to pay for a room for two nights."

Miz Bessie grinned and raised an eyebrow. "You two sharing?"

"If that's what's available, I'll take it," Joe agreed.

Grace looked at him with wide eyes. With rooms at a premium, it was usual for *cowboys* to bunk together. But from Miz Bessie's reaction, it seemed she'd got a different idea, and Grace could see how.

"Humph," Bessie muttered and looked her up and down. "You always acted like you was too high and mighty for that."

"Now, wait a minute," Joe protested. "I think you've misunderstood —"

"We're not sharing, not the two of us!" Grace burst out, her cheeks burning.

"You sure?" Miz Bessie leered at them. "No need for propriety here." Then her eyes narrowed. "Or are you trying to get out of paying my fee for entertaining gentlemen in your room?"

"We are not sharing a room," Grace said firmly.

"I meant I'm willing to share a room with other *men*," Joe emphasized, "if your rooms are full."

Miz Bessie folded her arms. "If you say so. I got one available room with two other gents, but if I find out you're sneaking off to her room," she said in a threatening tone, "you'll owe me triple the usual rate. And believe me, I got plenty of spies."

Grace was still flustered when they walked outside, and she was too embarrassed to look at Joe.

"I'm really sorry." Joe's voice was so low she barely

caught the words. "That was my fault. I didn't think properly . . ."

"Don't worry about it," Grace mumbled, trying to shake off her discomfort.

"Uh . . . so, to the sheriff's office?" Joe made it into a question, but the tone sounded more like a command.

She sighed but followed after Joe as he headed for the sheriff's office.

After listening to her story, Sheriff Shaw leaned back in his chair. "Well now, that sounds like a mighty fine piece of detective work, Miss Milton. Thing is, though, we can't investigate something that hasn't happened yet." His patronizing smile grated on Grace. "I will keep an ear out though."

"You don't think that pile by the train tracks is suspicious?" Joe asked.

"Could be some miner left it there."

"Why would a miner need logs?" Grace demanded.

The sheriff shrugged. "To secure a cave roof? Might even be planning to lay some tracks to bring a mining cart or train car in more easily. Who knows?"

"But it's right near the tracks. That's not logical. Maybe if I'd found it in the mountains . . ." Grace huffed out a breath.

Sheriff Shaw waved a dismissive hand. "Perhaps he got off the train late at night and didn't want his supplies stolen."

Grace clenched her teeth. A train didn't normally stop in a remote location like that. "So you're not going to investigate?"

"Like I say — can't call out a posse for a non-existent train robbery, and no point in sending anyone out to chase down the owner of the goods only to find out he's a miner. I'll surely take a look if you can bring me more *proof* of a train robbery, but —"

Pushing back her chair, Grace stood, cutting him off. "Thank you for your time, sheriff." She infused her words with tartness. "Guess I'll have to catch the train robbers myself."

"Whoa now, *if* a train robbery is about to happen — and that's a big 'if' — you shouldn't be foolish enough to get caught in the midst of it."

Grace was tired of people labeling her actions foolish or foolhardy. She'd caught those other criminals, and she'd catch these robbers with or without the sheriff's help. But before she could react, Joe leaned forward in his chair. "You have to admit this looks suspicious, Sheriff. Shouldn't you at least warn the engineers to be cautious?"

"Good idea, son. I'll do that."

Grace rolled her eyes — so if it came from a man, it was a good idea?

When they got outside the sheriff's office, she turned to Joe. "I told you he'd be no help," she said sharply.

He sighed. "I know. You were right."

"He doesn't even care that a robbery might take place!"

Joe took her arm. "Calm down. Look at it from his viewpoint — most of his lawmen are gone, helping out Deputy Clayton. He deals with crimes that have already happened."

"And he's worried about looking foolish if it's not connected with the outlaws." She stopped suddenly. "Unless he's in cahoots with them?" She marched down the street toward the railway station.

Joe caught up to her. "What would make you think that?"

"I don't trust the law round these parts, Joe. Where were they when . . . when my family was being killed? Look at Sheriff Behan, paid off by the Guiltless Gang like a common criminal!"

"Grace . . ."

She was hot with anger now. "Only one thing to do. I'll stop the holdup myself."

"Grace!"

She ignored him — his warning tone only increased her irritation. But with Joe close on her heels, Grace stomped along the wooden sidewalk, the planks ringing under her boots. "The first thing I need to do is talk to that ticket seller. Hopefully from speaking to him I'll be able to figure out which train the Andersens plan to hit."

But when they finally reached the stationhouse, the man behind the counter only shook his head when Grace described Wyatt Andersen. "I can't recall everyone who buys tickets and when, girl."

Grace pursed her lips. "Well, do you know anything about what's coming in or going out on the trains?"

The man shrugged. "Ain't any of my business."

"Please," she said. "This is important. This man killed my little sister." Her voice trembled, and Joe stepped closer and rested a reassuring hand on her shoulder. "And now I'm fairly certain he's planning a train robbery. He has to be stopped."

"A robbery?" The ticket master blanched and then rubbed his forehead. His eyes seemed to wander for a moment, and he cleared his throat. "Lost my only son to a train robbery only a few years back," he said, his voice softer now.

"If you can think of anything at all . . . anything special being transported in the next few days that might attract robbers?"

The ticket master stared out at the tracks as if inspecting each railway tie. He was silent for a while and then, after glancing around for other customers, he leaned over the counter and whispered, "I been told they picked the Watkins brothers for guarding that fugitive because there's a load of gold bars on that train too." Following another rapid scan of the platform, he continued, "Hearing the name Andersen reminds me of a story I heard in the saloon the other night. Someone said the Watkins brothers better guard their prisoner well 'cus old 'Iron Eyes' Andersen aimed to free him."

Joe's eyes bored into the older man's, shocked. "You sure about that?"

The ticket master spread his hands in an uncertain gesture. "Well, at the time I thought it was only saloon talk. You know how some men brag when they's full as a tick. For all I can tell, could be a lot of blow."

Drunk or not, gossip or not, it was the best clue they had. "Do you know which train has gold bars on it?" Grace said urgently.

"The next to come through Bisbee. Two days' time."

Grace's heart dropped as she realized — that was the train Caroline and Emily were due to take to go back East.

"Th-thank you for your help," she stuttered, thinking hard. She looked over at Joe. "As a matter of fact, can I buy a ticket for that train?"

Joe stared at her. "What are you —" he began.

"I have to be on it," she said, cutting him off.

"Well, hold me a ticket too," Joe said to the ticket master. "I may have to come along."

Grace turned startled eyes in his direction. "Joe —" She stopped herself and paid for her ticket. As soon as they got outside, they turned to one another.

"Grace, if those outlaws plan to rob the train and free the fugitive, they won't do it without a gunfight," Joe said, his eyes brimming with concern.

"That's why I have to stop them. I have to be on that train, Joe. It's my chance to capture two members of the Guiltless Gang, and . . ." She paused, her heart lurching with worry. "My friends are going to be on that train. I have to protect them, as best I can."

*   *   *

A short while later, Grace and Joe were still debating the dangers of her going on the train over dinner in the saloon when Sheriff Shaw strode in. She gritted her teeth when he settled at a nearby table, tipping his hat at her before removing it.

Joe leaned over and whispered, "Do you think knowing the possible link between the fugitive and the Andersens might change the sheriff's mind? And Shaw will know if there's gold on that train . . ."

"It's a waste of time," Grace insisted, but when Joe headed toward the sheriff's table she followed him. Joe told him about the possibility of the Andersens wanting to free the fugitive, and he nodded.

"You could be right," he mused.

"Then you'll have someone onboard the train to protect the passengers?" Grace asked hopefully.

The sheriff leaned back in his chair and stroked his chin. "Hmm. I recollect Deputy Clayton saying the Watkins brothers were transporting that fugitive." A relieved smile replaced the slight furrow over his brow. "They're the best bounty hunters in the state. We have nothing to worry about on that front."

Grace cringed at the sheriff's praise of the Watkinses and her hands curled into fists at her side. Those low-down varmints had stolen her bounty, and the sheriff trusted them to protect the train passengers? They couldn't be trusted to safeguard their own mother. She whirled and stalked from the saloon.

Joe followed after her. "I apologized for your abruptness," he said, giving her a sympathetic look, but his voice was stern. "I know you were steamed up in there, but you need to maintain cordial relations with law enforcement if you want to make a living as a bounty hunter. If they think you're an emotional, hysterical woman, they'll never rely on you to do a job."

Grace scuffed the toe of her boot in the dirt. As much as it pained her to admit it, Joe had a point. From now on, she'd keep her anger and frustration in check. It was tough enough to be taken seriously as a female bounty hunter.

"Hey," Joe said in a gentle voice. "I didn't mean to lecture you or hurt your feelings . . ."

"I know." Grace lifted her gaze from the puff of dust she'd stirred up to meet his eyes. "And you're right. I should have minded my manners."

Joe laughed. "I think that's the first time you've ever admitted I'm right about something. Maybe we could go for two in a row, and you could also say I was right about the sheriff handling the train robbery." He gave her a hopeful glance.

"Do you know who he's entrusting the train's safety to? Those Watkins brothers, they, they . . ." she spluttered, too angry to put together a coherent sentence. "Did I tell you how they stole my bounty?"

Grace launched into the story, and after she finished Joe was silent a moment. "No wonder you stalked out. I would have too. If I could get a hold of them, I'd wring their necks."

His voice was so menacing that Grace chuckled. "You and me both." She told him about shooting arrows at the brothers, and it was Joe's turn to laugh.

"You're priceless, Grace Milton. If anyone wants to know why I care for you so much, that's why." He grew sober for a moment, then added, "And for a million other reasons too."

Joe's eyes met hers and she tingled from head to toe. But when he bent to kiss her, she laid a firm hand on his chest to keep them apart. "No distractions when I have a job to do."

His sigh came from deep within his chest but he recovered rapidly and flashed her a brazen grin, inclining his head in a slight bow. "Yes, ma'am."

But as soon as she lowered her hand, he placed a quick kiss on her lips, pulling back a moment later. "Sorry," he said in a voice that sounded far from apologetic. "I couldn't resist."

"Be serious," Grace scolded, but she hadn't minded, of course. In fact, she was struggling to keep herself from flinging her arms around him and begging for another kiss. She reminded herself of the Andersens' possible train robbery, and the danger to Emily and Caroline, hoping it would lessen her desire.

"So, you intend to stop that train robbery yourself?" The flatness of Joe's words hinted at his disapproval.

"Someone has to."

"I really do understand your dislike of the Watkins brothers, but law enforcement trusts them. They should be able to handle a train robbery. Besides, we don't even know for sure that a robbery's going to occur."

"True, but I plan to be on that train if it does."

"Then I guess I will be taking that ticket being held for me. If you're going, so am I." When she shot him a withering glance, he only smiled and said, "Think of me as backup."

"But we can't go together. I told Caroline and Emily I might go with them, and Emily's been telling everyone in town I'm leaving. It's actually a really useful cover — it won't look like I'm bounty hunting. But if you're with me, it might start to raise questions . . ."

Joe pinched his lips together for a moment. "Fine, I'll board separately and stay undercover."

Grace just hoped they hadn't chosen the wrong train. If they had, she'd miss her chance to capture the Andersen twins — they'd get away with it all over again.

And innocent passengers might die.

CHAPTER 21

Two days later, Emily danced down the street, holding Grace's hand and dragging her along. Caroline attempted to keep pace but, weighed down under the burden of all her luggage, she soon trailed behind. Grace had insisted on carrying some of Caroline's bags in addition to her saddlebag. She'd quietly paid to stable Bullet for a few days, though the stable hands hadn't been exactly welcoming. But Bullet had calmed down quite a bit when Joe led Paint into the adjoining stall.

Standing on the platform, Grace fidgeted in the walking dress Caroline had insisted on giving her in thanks for their tickets. Used to looser calicos or Ndeh buckskin clothing, Grace chafed in the multi-layered dress with a pleated overskirt that draped across the front and met in a set of low hip tucks on either side. Suede high-button boots and a hat with feathers completed her outfit. Caroline had tried to talk her into a dress with a bustle, but Grace declined. She needed to be able to move freely. This dress was restricting enough, but it did have one advantage — the puffiness at each side allowed her to conceal her gun easily, and no one would suspect that in her saddlebag she carried coils of rope, a knife, and bullets, or that she planned to apprehend some of the most wanted criminals in the state.

Grace spied Joe further down the platform leaning against a wooden post, acting nonchalant. He gawked for a moment when he saw her, grinned, and winked. Then, obviously recalling their plan, he resumed his casual, uninterested air. Although they weren't traveling together, she had to admit that knowing that Joe would be on the train gave her a feeling of comfort.

Grace tried to keep up with Emily's non-stop chatter, but all she could think about was the fugitive, the Andersen twins, the Watkins brothers . . . Her main worry was whether the Andersens were working alone or if other members of the Guiltless Gang would assist them with the robbery. Much as she'd love to apprehend other members of the gang, the more there were, the more difficult it could be to take them on. Although they'd cheated her out of her reward money, Grace assumed the Watkins brothers would at least be helping to capture the train robbers, and she reminded herself that she had Joe for additional backup. Together they should be able to subdue the criminals, she told herself firmly. As long as she'd chosen the correct train . . .

Emily tugged at her hand. "Are you listening?"

Grace forced her attention back to the small girl, who was bobbing up and down with excitement. "What did you say, sweetheart?"

"I asked if you would want to come and visit me at my grandma's house."

"I'd love to," Grace answered, but guilt pooled in the pit of her stomach where fear had already made it tense. She hoped she'd be able to keep her hurried breakfast down once she boarded the train.

"Ma!" Emily called eagerly at Caroline, huffing and puffing her way toward them. "Grace is going to visit us back East."

Her mother beamed and plopped her bags beside the ones Grace had carried. "We'd love to have you," she said, catching her breath.

That made Grace feel even worse. She hadn't exactly lied — she would love to visit Emily and Caroline, but the half-truth that hung between them added to her remorse. She'd miss them both, but she had to hide that sorrow as well as conceal her true purpose.

"Where's your family located?" Caroline asked.

Grace took a deep breath and swallowed the lump rising in her throat.

Caroline clapped a hand to her mouth, then reached over to touch her arm. "Oh, sweetie, I'm so sorry. I didn't mean to —"

"It's all right," Grace said, her voice shaking a little.

"How about we talk about something else," Caroline suggested to Emily, and Grace felt a wash of relief. "Why don't you take a peek to see if you can spy the train arriving?"

Emily rolled her eyes exaggeratedly. "I don't need to look — I hear it. Listen."

In the distance, the train rumbled toward them, belching plumes of smoke. Metal screeching, the engine finally shuddered to a stop and the platform launched into action. Men shouted and loaded cars, while passengers milled toward the two carriages. The conductor jumped onto the platform and tried to organize the disorderly crowd. "Luggage in the first combination car," he shouted, but most people ignored him, clinging to their possessions as they boarded.

Grace helped Emily up the steps of the nearest carriage and found two seats across from each other, plopping herself quickly into the window seat and gratefully taking off her hat. She needed to keep Emily away from the windows if any shooting started. The girl pouted for a second but then sat in the aisle seat, and her mother squeezed into the space opposite them, piling her bags under both Emily's and her own feet.

"This is so exciting!" Emily said, squeezing Grace's hand. "It's the best day ever."

Grace hoped for her sake that the small girl was right and their ride would be uneventful and fun, but inside she quivered with anticipation and dread. The next station was two hours away but she estimated the hidden supplies had been stashed about an hour from town.

She stole a glance around the carriage but saw no sign of the Watkins brothers or the fugitive. She wasn't sure if they'd be in the other passenger car, or perhaps in a secure carriage, possibly with the gold, and she had no real idea how to find out.

Beside her, Emily was chattering away to the other passengers. Maybe one of them would know, or had seen something? But if Grace asked too many questions, she might raise people's suspicions.

The train whistle blew and Emily covered her ears, and as the carriage lurched forward the young girl clutched Grace's arm. Caroline leaned across the aisle to pat Emily's shoulder. "It's all right, honey. The train's just starting up." She had to shout to be heard over the thump of the engine, the squealing of metal, and the jolting of carriages bumping back and forth.

"Are you sure?" Emily's face had gone pale.

"We're fine," Grace reassured her. "I remember how

frightened I was the first time I rode a train, and I was much older than you are now."

Emily's eyes widened. "Really? You were scared?" When Grace nodded, she sat up straighter. "I'm going to be as brave as you then."

Grace smiled at her. "You're very, very brave," she said with a laugh — and it was true. If she managed to apprehend the Andersen twins, it all would be thanks to Emily's keen observations.

When the conductor came through to check tickets, Grace tried to quiz him, feigning innocence, about the different carriages on the train. He smiled indulgently and answered her questions, listing the various cars, most of which were hopper cars carrying silver or other minerals from the mines, or boxcars filled with cargo. Then he mentioned the combine.

"What's that?" Emily asked, and Grace glanced at her, thankful the little girl was asking questions now — it deflected some of the pressure off her.

"Well, miss," the conductor said with a friendly smile. "The combine carries both cargo and passengers. People sometimes store their luggage there. Big shipments can go there too."

"Like what?" Emily asked. Grace smiled.

"Oh, mail and such. And other important things." He leaned in with a conspiratorial smile. "Sometimes secret things."

He started to move on but Emily stopped him. "Are there secret things on *this* train? I'm good at keeping secrets, aren't I, Grace?" She turned to her with wide, innocent eyes for confirmation.

"Very good at it," Grace said, wanting to squeeze her in thanks, even if she didn't know how helpful she was truly being.

The conductor winked at Emily. "Some secrets are better kept private, young lady."

"That's the car at the end of the train, right?" Grace tried to make her question sound harmless.

"Yep, they go at the rear. Usually we only have one of those, but today we got two."

"How come?" Emily asked the question that was on the tip of Grace's tongue. They made a good team. The conductor had a cagey look in his eyes when he answered. "Like I said, some things are best kept private."

In spite of that, Grace had got the information she needed. If the gold and the fugitive were on the train, they must both be in the combine car. Now her only problems were to work out which of the two cars they were in, and how to get in there so she would be ready for the attack.

A few people strolled the aisles, stretching their legs. Maybe she could do the same? But none of them left the carriage and she worried she would look suspicious, especially as a woman alone. Still, she couldn't wait much longer — they'd shortly be getting to that isolated spot where she'd uncovered the supplies.

Grace stood and moved into the aisle, holding on to the seat back as the train swayed from side to side. "I'm feeling a bit cramped. I'll just walk around for a bit."

"Oh, I'm so sorry, Grace," Caroline said. "Our luggage is taking up too much room. I'll hold some of it on my lap —"

"Please, don't worry. I have plenty of room. I'm just not used to sitting much — except on horseback, that is," she said with a smile.

"I understand completely. It's such a luxury for me to sit during the day." Caroline sank back onto the seat. "I'm enjoying every minute. I can barely keep my eyes open."

Emily pulled at Grace's arm. "Can I come with you?"

"Why don't you stay with your ma? When I come back, maybe we can play a game."

Caroline leaned across the aisle. "Come on, sweetie, let Grace have a break. She's been listening to your chatter since we arrived at the station," she said to her daughter with a smile.

Emily thrust out her lower lip and crossed her arms.

Grace bent over and whispered, "Why don't you play detective while I'm gone? See if you can find out where all the passengers are headed." She hoped that would keep the little girl occupied for a while. She staggered to the front of the carriage, trying to keep her balance. Joe was seated in the same car, close to the door, and he looked up as she passed, raising his eyebrows subtly at her outfit. She smiled back, pursing her lips ruefully, but when he started to stand she shook her head. He gave her a questioning look but sank back into his seat.

Not yet, she mouthed.

Joe nodded a little, drifting his eyes closed as if he were falling asleep, but Grace could see that his eyes were open a slit.

Once she had become used to the train's rocking motion, Grace walked from one end of the carriage to the other and back again to make sure that she didn't seem to be heading anywhere too specific. When she passed, Emily was busy questioning an elderly man. Grace strolled back down the aisle again. This time when she reached the rear of the car, she peeked into the next one — but instead of windows, a wooden door covered the opening. *That must be one of the combines*, she thought with a leap of hopefulness. But how could she sneak into the car if she couldn't see in? Anything — or anyone — could be in there.

Grace glanced around to see if any of the passengers were watching, and when she was sure she was unobserved, she tugged open the door and stepped out onto the platform between carriages. Wind rushed past and she grabbed the metal railing as the train swung around a curve. Between the wind and the pull of the train's momentum, she could barely stand, and she clung to the metal bar as the train tilted and swayed.

When the tracks straightened out and Grace could stand upright, she stepped across the gap, the track beneath her whizzing by at a dizzying speed, and clutched the handrail on the other side. She pulled at the heavy door to the next carriage, but it didn't budge. Afraid it might be locked, she pushed down on the metal handle again and yanked.

This time the door slid open so fast, her feet skidded across the metal platform and she almost lost her balance. Grace hung on to the handle and scrambled for a foothold as the train tilted the other way. Before the door could slam back into place, she stuck a foot into the opening and then squeezed her body through.

She found herself in a car piled high with luggage. Peering around each stack to be sure no one was there, she weaved her way through the towering piles of bags. Thankfully, the Watkins brothers and the fugitive weren't in this carriage when she'd made her noisy entry. Then she realized that if they were here, they must be in the final car. But getting that next door open without being noticed was going to be nearly impossible . . .

Behind her, the carriage door opened and then slammed shut again, and someone shuffled behind the heaps of luggage. Grace jumped and turned, one hand sliding under the apron folds of her skirt to reach her concealed holster.

Heart racing, she stood rigid, watching, waiting. Whoever entered made no further move. Had it only been bags sliding along the floor? Grace had almost convinced herself it had been her imagination, when a head peeked around the largest pile of luggage.

CHAPTER 22

"Emily!" Grace cried. "You shouldn't be following me. What are you doing here? You need to go back to your mother. Now."

The girl's lip trembled at the sharpness in Grace's voice. "I-I want to help you. Are you looking for outlaws?" She glanced around. "There's nobody here," she said.

Grace headed toward her. "Never mind what I'm doing. We need to get you back to your mother." She grabbed Emily's hand and pulled her toward the door.

The girl dug in her heels. "I'm practicing being a bounty hunter like you!"

"I know, but you need to go back to your ma. She'll worry."

Emily twisted away. "No, she won't. She fell asleep! So I can help you."

"There's nothing to do here." Grace waved a shaky hand toward the mound of luggage. "Look, there's no one in this carriage. We need to just go back to our seats."

Her heart raced even faster as she shoved back the door and stepped out onto the platform. She gripped Emily's hand and tried to steady them both on the narrow shelf of metal. The gap between it and the other side looked too wide for Emily to cross safely.

"How did you get across here?" Grace had to shout to make herself heard above the clatter of the wheels.

"I jumped."

Emily's matter-of-fact answer left Grace speechless. If Caroline knew what her daughter had been doing, she would have been horrified. Emily could have fallen between the carriages and been crushed to death.

Suddenly, the wheels squealed along the tracks, and they clung on tight as the train jolted and shuddered to an unexpected stop, throwing Grace and Emily back against the door. The gap between carriages looked less scary now that the train had stopped, but they were in the middle of nowhere, with nothing but desert scrub all around. A jolt of dread went through Grace.

They must have reached the ambush spot already.

Emily frowned. "What's wrong, Grace? Why are we stopping here? There's no station . . ."

"Let's go." Grace's voice cracked like a whip. She had to get Emily to her mother.

But before they could step onto the other platform, someone screamed in the passenger car.

They couldn't go back in there; it could be dangerous.

Grace fumbled back behind her for the door handle to the luggage car and managed to slide it open wide enough for Emily to fit.

"Crawl back in there, Emily, and hide behind the suitcases."

"What's happening?"

"I don't know yet," Grace said quickly. "Just, please, do as I say."

She followed the little girl into the luggage car and slammed the door shut. She crept behind a mound of suitcases beside Emily. The young girl was shaking now, and Grace wrapped an arm around her. "I need you to listen very carefully," she whispered. "Whatever happens, I want you to stay here. Don't let anyone see you and don't make a sound. Do you understand?"

Eyes wide, face pale, Emily nodded. "Is it the outlaws?"

Grace took a breath. "I think so, and I may need to leave you. I want you to promise to stay here and not move."

"I want to come with you. I can help —"

"Emily, remember when we talked about being brave? Staying here is hard, but I know you can do it."

Emily pinched her lips together glumly — but just then the door to their compartment banged open and four men charged in, bandanas covering their mouths, hats pulled low over their eyes, guns drawn. Grace clapped a hand over Emily's mouth to smother the rest of the girl's words. Then she caught the girl's eye and shook her head, warning Emily to stay silent. She nodded vigorously, and Grace slowly removed her hand.

One man motioned behind him and barked out, "Take care of the other passenger cars."

Two men rushed out of the door, and the other two men headed for the last carriage that Grace hadn't been able to investigate. As soon as she heard that door bang open and a shot ring out, she jumped to her feet. Bending close to Emily's ear, she whispered, "Stay hidden. Don't move or make a sound until I come back for you. Do you understand?"

Emily nodded. "Be careful, Grace." Her voice was so quiet she could barely hear it.

"Be brave."

"I will," Emily mouthed. "I promise."

CHAPTER 23

Grace rounded the pile of luggage and headed toward the gunshot in the other combine car. Joe was still in the passenger carriage. She'd have to trust him to take care of the people in there as best he could, and she just hoped that those two thugs had no plans to hurt innocent bystanders. Most likely they'd been sent to keep the passengers from interfering with the gang's mission — the gold theft and prison break.

Ahead of her, the door to the other combine car remained partially ajar. She stealthily darted behind one stack of luggage after another, and when she reached the door at the end of the car, she peeked around it. Across the gap, the metal door of the next carriage had been pried with a crowbar and stood partway open. She'd be exposed out on the platform between the carriages if the outlaws returned . . . Grace took a deep breath to calm her fluttering nerves. *You can do this*, she told herself, and stepped across the gap, keeping to one side so no one inside the next carriage could see her.

She peered through the opening. Stacks of wooden boxes blocked her view. This had to be the car. It was the last one on the train. If only she could see better . . .

Grunts and slams came from beyond the boxes, and cautiously Grace grasped the bent door and pulled, but it stayed stuck. Reluctant to make a noise and draw attention to herself, she knelt and slid her fingers into the opening, then tugged on it with all her might. The door creaked open a few inches. Grace froze and listened, her hand on her gun. When the thumps and groans continued, she tried again. This time the door slid a little further, wide enough to squeeze inside — but as she did so, she came face to face with a wall of boxes. The robbers must have shoved them there to prevent anyone from disturbing them. From the sounds inside, someone was getting slammed around, and something heavy was being dragged across the floor.

Grace whipped out her gun and flattened herself against the door, waiting for someone to come rushing out. After a few harrowing minutes, when no one did, she slid her gun back into her holster, adjusted her dress folds so they covered it, and bunched up her skirts in each hand so she could creep further into the carriage. Crouching low, she hid behind the boxes. If they noticed movement, they were likely to shoot at normal head or heart height. It'd take a second for them to glance down, and by then she'd have the advantage. Joe had taught her the fast draw, and she could whip out her gun and fire in one fluid movement.

But first she needed to find out what exactly was going on.

She crawled past the first stack of boxes, which was blocking the light. Peeking around the nearest one, she spotted the Andersen brothers and couldn't help her disgusted grimace at the sight of the men who'd been part of the gang that slaughtered her family. She'd been thinking about their faces every night, and now here they were in front of her, in the flesh. Her fingers itched as they hovered near her gun.

Bandana down, Wyatt, with his patchy beard and pockmarked face, stood over a badly battered Frank Watkins, gun pointed at his heart. Grace longed to yank out her own revolver and pull the trigger, but Joe's warning about her temper came back to her. She mustn't do something foolish, something that would give away her presence. She choked back the bile rising in her throat and forced herself to concentrate on the rest of the scene.

Nearby, an almost identical replica of Wyatt, but with smoother skin and minus the scraggy beard, knelt over Asa Watkins, securing his arms with rope. The other two

Watkins brothers had been shot. Wade lay face up, eyes closed, blood streaming from his shoulder, drawing in shuddery, irregular breaths. Steven, barely breathing, was sprawled face down, a pool of blood surrounding his left hip and leg. They'd been taken by surprise. Grace fought back the nightmares that threatened to engulf her at the sight of the blood . . .

She'd accounted for the Andersen twins and the Watkins brothers, but where was the convict they were guarding? Just then, the train carriage shook and tilted to one side as a heavy-set man, his chin blackened with stubble, climbed the stairs at the back of the train. He stomped into the carriage, wiped the sweat from his brow with the kerchief around his neck, and grabbed a heavy wooden box.

He shot a dirty look at Wyatt and his twin. "I could use some help here."

Wyatt growled back, "Soon as we're done tying up these bounty hunters."

"I'm breaking my back here while you pretty boys fool around with a simple job."

"Shut up, Clarence," Wyatt snapped. "You'd be looking at thirty years if it wasn't for us."

Clarence must be the fugitive — and Grace realized that the Watkins brothers weren't going to be much help capturing the outlaws. No matter how fast she shot, she'd never be able to take out all three criminals without getting herself injured or killed. She'd only get off one shot before the other two outlaws fired at her, and it would be a full-on shoot-out. Grace gritted her teeth, trying to think of a plan as Clarence staggered to the door with the box.

"I can't drag that safe outta here on my own."

"Come on, Nat," Wyatt snapped. "We don't got much time here. If that engineer comes to and they get those logs cleared from the track, the train'll take off."

Clarence turned and, his voice filled with disdain, said, "You're fools for not killing him."

"Told Nat to finish him off, but maybe he's too afraid of swinging from the gallows." Wyatt pitched his voice high and mocking. "You don't hurry, you gonna be feeling that noose around yer neck."

Nat glared at his brother. "You wanna tie him up? Go right ahead. He's flopping around like a fish." Nat yanked on the rope binding Asa's hands and he yelped, kicking and bucking until Nat kneed him in the back. Then the Andersen twin wrapped rope around Asa's ankles and stuffed his own bandana in his mouth, wrenching it so hard that Asa's head jerked up and back.

Just then, Asa's gaze met Grace's and his eyes widened. Like her father had done when she'd been hidden in the root cellar, Grace signaled him with her eyes not to give her away, and his slight nod indicated he understood.

Nat stepped over Asa and flipped Frank Watkins onto his back. Flat on his belly, Asa twisted his head to the side to watch his brother being trussed, and the two brothers made eye contact. Asa lifted his brows and signaled Frank with a quick, small toss of his head that Grace was there.

Grace clenched her teeth. She thought he'd understood her signal not to give her away, but when Frank didn't get the message, Asa continued to wiggle his eyebrows and flick his head in her direction, increasingly unsubtle. Frank's knitted brow indicated he still hadn't interpreted the message.

But Wyatt Andersen did.

"Someone there?" he demanded, whipping his head around in Grace's direction. As she'd expected, his gaze went way over her head and he examined the boxes high above where she crouched. She pulled her head back like a turtle curling inside its shell and held her breath, grasping her gun. But when he didn't approach, she risked peering around the corner again. Wyatt stood with his back to her, gun aimed at Frank. The boxes concealed her now, but if the outlaws planned to unload all of them, she'd be exposed. She had to find a way to stop them before that happened.

When Clarence stomped out of the carriage again, the odds became two to one. If only Grace could see where he went, she could judge how long she had before he returned — if she timed it right, she could try taking out both of the Andersen twins while he was gone. But hadn't Clarence said he was waiting for their help? If she waited until one of the twins went to help too, she could shoot the remaining brother, then pick off the others as they re-entered the car, hopefully while they were carrying the heavy boxes and wouldn't have time to get to their weapons.

As Grace watched, Wyatt nudged his brother with the toe of his boot. "Hurry up and get out there. Faster we get that cart loaded, the quicker we can get outta here before the law arrives."

"No law out here. We seen to that. Quit your carping, Wyatt." Rope in hand, Nat sat back on his heels. "You could get out there and help him yourself."

Wyatt shook his head. "Someone needs to guard these prisoners."

Nat snarled so low and menacingly, he sounded like a dog about to attack. He turned a hate-filled glance on his brother. "You don't have any intention of helping out, do you? You always was lazy."

Wyatt's laugh was sinister and threatening. "But I have the brains. Something you ain't got. Who was it planned all this?"

While the brothers argued, Grace saw Frank's hand snake out, scrabbling for the loose gun lying just out of reach.

"You fool," Wyatt screeched as he suddenly spotted the movement. "While you're arguing, he's going for his gun!" He strode over and kicked the weapon out of reach, but as he passed, Frank grabbed for his ankle. Wyatt sidestepped his grasping hands, lifted his boot, and brought his heel down on Frank's outstretched wrist with so much force bones crunched. Frank screamed in agony.

"That'll teach you." Wyatt walked past his brother and cuffed him on the ear. "Get his wrists bound, now!"

Nat grabbed Frank's wrists and yanked them toward his back, leaning down and planting his knee on Frank's back to wrap the rope around them. Frank screamed in pain but Nat just laughed. The Watkins brother's eyes rolled back in his head and he looked as if he'd passed out, but when Nat yanked his head back to put the gag in place, Frank looked up. Right at Grace. He gasped, finally realizing what his brother had been indicating, and twitched his head from side to side, trying to get a better look.

"What you staring at?" Wyatt demanded. "Sully and Pete should have secured the other carriages. We took care of the conductor and engineer and fireman. No one else to worry about, is there?"

He nudged Asa with his foot. "You don't have no backup on this train, do you? No Feds or deputies?"

Asa shook his head.

Wyatt turned and stalked in Grace's direction. "Better check it out. Can't take risks."

Grace pulled back to hide, but in her haste she cracked her elbow against a box.

"What was that?" Wyatt shouted. "Someone's there."

Her elbow stung so badly tears sprang to Grace's eyes. She rubbed her arm to ease the pain, her heart pounding as heavy footsteps rushed toward her.

Before she could reach her gun, Wyatt Andersen grabbed her by the scruff of her neck and dragged her out from behind the boxes.

CHAPTER 24

"Well, well, well, what is this?" Wyatt lifted Grace off her feet.

She trembled, searching her brain for a believable excuse. "I-I was looking for my sister."

"And just why would your sister be in here?"

"We were playing hide-and-seek. I thought she might be behind these boxes."

"And is she?" Wyatt towered over her to glance into the dark corners.

"N-no, sir. She must have slipped by me into another carriage." Grace felt the side of her dress, making sure her revolver was concealed under the apron folds. If her gun showed, she'd give herself away.

Wyatt hauled her roughly to her feet. "I'll take you back to the passenger car where you belong."

Nat interrupted. "She seen us, Wyatt. Makes no sense to let her go. We don't need no witnesses . . ."

"Huh, so you do got some brains after all." Wyatt gave his brother an evil grin. "We'll take care of her, but right now we don't need no more bodies in our way here. Hard 'nuff to get the stuff loaded as it is, with such slow progress."

Nat scowled. "Why should I hurry? I do the dirty mule work while you play around with little girls?"

Wyatt's low growl turned Grace's stomach, and being this close to him was making her want to vomit. She tensed as his hand tightened on her arm — the one she used to shoot. If only she'd had her gun out and ready, she could have fired the moment he spotted her, but she'd missed her chance. She wanted to turn on him, to cause him the same pain she'd felt when he and the gang killed her family.

Wyatt shoved Grace ahead of him out of the carriage, across the platform and through the next car, all the while grumbling about her keeping him from his work. She kept silent. They were alone in the second combine car, where she knew Emily was still hiding. If only she could reach her gun. Grace prayed that the little girl would stay silent and hidden — but when Wyatt dragged her past Emily's hiding place, she gasped.

Grace froze.

Wyatt halted. "What was that?"

"I-I didn't hear anything," she lied. She hoped her trembling wasn't obvious. *Please, please, Em, stay silent. Don't move.*

But Wyatt dragged Grace toward the sound, then stopped and glared at the small girl crouched behind the boxes.

She begged Emily with her eyes to remain silent, but the girl's teeth were chattering so hard she couldn't have got a word out. Tucking his gun into his holster, Wyatt used his other hand to grab Emily roughly and drag her out.

"This your sister?" he demanded.

"Yes," Grace squeaked out at the same time as Emily shook her head.

"I don't have time for games. Is she or ain't she?"

"Yes, yes she is."

Wyatt dragged both of them toward the passenger car. "Sully, he's good with kids." His menacing laugh told a different story. "He'll know *just* what to do with you two."

When they reached the door, he nudged Grace hard. "Open that there door," he commanded, but she struggled with it. His sharp elbow connected with her ribs. "Move it!"

If he poked her any lower, he'd feel the gun. Panic rising within her, Grace jerked on the door with all her strength.

It slid partway open, but not enough for all three of them to exit.

"Wider," Wyatt barked.

"I'm trying," Grace whimpered. "I'm not used to such heavy doors." She hoped she sounded convincingly weak and helpless so he wouldn't see her as a threat.

"Try harder," Wyatt said, slamming a knee into her backside.

Grace yanked on the door again and it slid wide open so fast she stumbled and almost fell. Wyatt jerked on her arm to pull her upright and ordered her out onto the platform. He pulled Emily to the edge.

"Jump," he snarled when she stood there trembling.

"Try, Em, please," Grace pleaded.

But before Emily could comply, Wyatt picked her up and tossed her to the opposite side. Emily's head banged against the door of the passenger car, and she wailed, crumpling like a rag doll.

"Quit your sniveling before I put a bullet through you." Wyatt stepped across and grabbed her arm, hauling her to her feet.

"Be brave, Em," Grace begged. But inside, her temper was burning hot. She'd find a way to make this man pay as soon as he let go of her arm. Wyatt's fingers dug in more deeply when they reached the passenger car. "Open it. And don't try no funny business or I'll throw your sister from the train."

Abby's face floated before Grace's eyes in a fury-filled cloud, blocking her vision and making it hard to breathe. Only the thought of Emily, helpless, her body broken and battered on the ground below the train kept Grace silent. She pulled the door open and marched into the passenger car, with Wyatt clenching her arm and dragging Emily behind.

Wyatt called to the man who was guarding the passengers. "Sully, keep an eye on these two girls. Remember their faces, 'cus they're gonna get the special treatment."

Grace gulped. He wouldn't kill them in front of witnesses, but later . . .

Caroline caught sight of her daughter and screamed. "Emily! My baby! Let her go!"

The woman beside her grasped her arm to prevent Emily's mother from charging down the aisle. Caroline shook away the restraint desperately, and hearing her mother's voice, Emily started screaming and wriggling frantically. She jerked loose from Wyatt's grasp, and he shoved her hard, sending her stumbling. She fell face-down in the aisle. Wyatt glowered at both Emily and Caroline.

"Calm that brat down," he shouted at Caroline.

An elderly man pushed himself to his feet, his face red and contorted with anger. The bowler hat on his lap tumbled to the floor. He leaned on his cane and strode toward Wyatt. "You can't treat children this way. Let that girl go at once or I'll —"

When the old man lifted his cane to strike, Wyatt shoved Grace aside roughly. She lost her balance and tumbled into a woman's lap, her gun arm trapped underneath her, her boot heels tangled in her skirt layers. With a roar, Wyatt ducked the feeble blow from the man's cane and came in low, knocking him to the ground. The old man lay on his back like an overturned beetle, his arms and legs jerking uselessly in the air, but he still tried to whack Wyatt's legs with the cane.

Wyatt stood, whipped out his gun, and took aim.

"No, no, don't shoot." The old man's words were high and squeaky with fear.

The Andersen twin didn't even blink. He pulled the trigger and the report threw the man back hard against the floor. Blood splattered the front of his waistcoat and air gurgled out of the man's lungs. A dull look appeared in his eyes before they closed.

Everyone went deathly silent. Even Emily.

Sicker than she'd ever been, Grace stared at the old man's chest, willing him to breathe. A tiny shudder went through him.

The door to the compartment banged open and Joe burst through, one hand on his holster.

"Grace?" he called, his voice tight. He scanned the carriage until his eyes fell on her. "Are you all right?"

No, she wasn't all right, but Joe needed reassurance, not her fears. "I-I'm fine," she choked out.

"Stay where you are," Wyatt barked at Joe. "Hands in the air." He yanked Grace up from the seat and dragged her in front of him like a shield. "Or I'll kill her."

When Joe hesitated, Wyatt put his pistol to Grace's head. Joe slowly raised his hands.

With the cold metal pressed against her temple, Grace went into a deeper, darker place than she'd ever gone before. Wyatt could kill her, but she'd never let him kill Joe, Emily, or Caroline. None of these innocent people. She gritted her teeth as rage built inside her. She'd do whatever she had to do to take him down. Snaking her hand under the decorative panel of fabric at her hips, her fingers closed around the gun.

"Sully, get over there and take his weapon," Wyatt ordered, indicating to Joe. "And nobody else get any bright ideas of being a hero."

As he spoke, Emily caught Grace's eye. The small girl was moving toward Sully.

No! Grace wanted to scream, but she couldn't call Wyatt's attention to the little girl or he'd surely shoot her too.

Suddenly Emily shrieked and threw herself on the floor in front of Sully's feet, kicking and screaming as if she were having a full-blown temper tantrum. Sully tripped over her and fell, his gun skittering across the floor.

Wyatt's gun hand wavered.

That second was all Grace needed.

"Get down," she screamed at the passengers as she twisted out of Wyatt's grip and drew her gun. Afraid her shot might go wild while they struggled, she slammed the revolver's butt against Wyatt's temple. His head snapped to the side and he collapsed in a heap.

At the same time, Joe rushed over to the struggling Sully, his gun pointed. He jerked the man off Emily and wrenched his hands behind his back. "Someone toss me a rope," he yelled.

But before anyone could respond, the door to the compartment slammed open again and the outlaw guarding the other passenger car burst through the doorway, gun drawn. Grace whipped her gun up and pulled the trigger. Her shot caught him in the shoulder of his gun arm, and the outlaw crumpled to the floor.

A man sitting nearby tackled the sprawling man and snatched the gun from his hand. Then he picked up Sully's gun and pointed both weapons at the struggling outlaw. "I'll keep him covered until someone ties him up."

Grace bent to pull the pistol from Wyatt Andersen's limp hand. Her stomach churned as her fingers brushed the hand of that murderer, but at last he lay helpless at her feet. She could put a bullet through his heart. He deserved it . . .

With his gun in her left hand, Grace stood and pointed her own revolver at Wyatt's chest. The revolver that had belonged to her father.

A short distance away, Emily struggled to her feet, dusted herself off, and gave Grace a triumphant smile. "You got him. He's one of the men from the poster, isn't he? What are you going to do now?"

Grace swallowed hard. Here was her chance. But Emily was watching her, supposedly learning how to be a bounty hunter. If she shot Wyatt, what would she teach Emily about justice and revenge?

She tightened her finger on the trigger.

CHAPTER 25

Through the tears misting her eyes, Grace loosened her trigger finger and returned a tremulous smile. "I-I'm going to turn him in," she answered the young girl, lowering her gun.

"I need rope," Joe yelled again.

A cowboy near the back of the car hopped up. "I got some in the luggage car. I can get it."

"No." Grace's voice cracked through the air. Nat and Clarence were back there. "I have rope in my bag." She handed Wyatt's gun to the cowboy, and he tipped his hat and took it. "Make sure he doesn't move," she said, indicating the Andersen twin.

The cowboy trained his gun on Wyatt but said, "Don't

think I'll be needing to use this. You did a right good job of knocking him out."

That had been due to Joe's training. When he'd taught her tracking, he'd demonstrated several ways of overpowering enemies with blows to the head or neck. She'd been lucky to hit the right spot.

Grace strode over, ruffled Emily's hair, and whispered, "Fast thinking." Then she opened her saddlebag and tossed rope to Joe and the man who was guarding the other outlaw.

The passengers stared in shock as Grace strapped a knife around her waist, tossed another coil of rope over her shoulder, and strode off, gun drawn.

Wyatt had left all the doors open, making her passage through the cars easier, but she hid behind each doorway and glanced around inside before entering the carriages. Nat or Clarence might come to find out why Wyatt hadn't returned.

When Grace reached the second combine car, she stood outside and listened. The carriage rocked from side to side — someone was either exiting or boarding. The sounds of cursing grew fainter and so she deduced they must be leaving.

She slipped behind the stack of boxes. The piles had grown much shorter, and they barely hid her when she crouched. Nat and Clarence must have carried most of them out. When she didn't hear a sound, except for groaning, Grace ventured a quick look. Wade Watkins was thrashing, but his eyes were still closed. Frank's forehead rested on the floor. Had he passed out from pain? Or was it too hard for him to watch the fugitive he'd been guarding make off with the loot? She waved to catch Asa's attention. The startled, wary look in his eyes turned to shock when he caught sight of her — no doubt surprised she'd made it back there.

The cursing outside the train grew louder and Grace signaled Asa to wait. She had no idea how long the outlaws took transporting each load. She'd stay hidden and watch and wait as they carried out the next load to give her an idea of timing. The train carriage tipped to one side and the cursing grew louder. Grace ducked behind the boxes.

"Where's your damned brother?" Clarence growled as they re-entered. "He planning to help at all?"

Nat's tone was bitter. "Like I said, guess he don't feel the need to do any of the dirty work."

Clarence stomped across the floor close to Grace's hiding spot. "No telling how soon the engineer might come around. Maybe we should move that next." He gestured toward the metal safe just a few feet away from her.

She scuttled around the boxes so she'd be hidden from view.

"Looks like it'll take both of us to move it," said Nat.

The two men grunted as they heaved the box. A loud

clunk shook the floor, and Clarence cursed up a storm. Thumps and more curses were followed by a loud scraping sound.

"If you keep being so clumsy we might not need to dynamite this safe." The sarcastic edge to Clarence's voice had an angry bite.

"It slipped." Nat's tone was a mix of anger and frustration. "We shoulda waited for Wyatt. What's keeping him, anyway?"

"All he had to do was take two little girls to the passenger car."

"What if the engineer woke up?"

"Then he'd likely start this train, not chase after Wyatt."

"I'm telling you, this ain't like Wyatt . . ."

"Quit yer jawing and grab your end again."

Nat heaved a sigh. Then, with a moan louder than the ones coming from Wade, he heaved the safe. "What's *in* this thing?"

"Supposed to be filled with gold bars." Clarence huffed between words.

"You go out the door first," Nat commanded.

"Yeah, so's I have to go down the steps backward?"

Nat's answer was muffled.

Grace waited until the carriage tilted under their weight, then she raced over, yanked out her knife, and cut the ropes binding Asa.

"We don't have much time," she whispered as she undid

his gag. "If one of us stands at each side of the door, we can surprise them when they're coming through."

"What about untying Frank?" Asa rubbed his wrists and ankles, which had turned blue. He tottered to his feet, shaking his arms.

"We don't have time. I don't know how long we have before they return. Once we've captured them, we'll take care of Frank. His arm is useless for shooting."

Frank lifted his head and his eyes bored into hers. The rage in them didn't bode well for when he was untied, and Grace was grateful he was gagged.

"Get your gun," she ordered, ignoring him, "and pick up Frank's so they can't use it."

Asa glared at her mutinously. "I don't take orders from women."

"Fine, suit yourself," Grace said as she bent to scoop up Frank's gun.

Asa elbowed her out of the way. "I got it." With a snort, he stood. "You take that side of the door. I'll take this one."

Grace didn't take kindly to being ordered around either, but she wasn't going to let Asa's ego jeopardize this capture. He took up the position with the best vantage point, and she took the other.

"Wait until they both get through the door," Grace said. "If we shoot too soon, the other one will get away."

The carriage tilted.

"They're coming," Asa mouthed.

Grace nodded. She'd already figured that out. But rather than waiting as planned, Asa charged out and fired immediately. Grace was on the wrong side of the door to see around the corner, and she ducked as another shot rang out. Asa flew off the narrow platform and onto the train tracks below. His gun discharged when he landed, and the bullet pinged into the metal under the train.

He screamed, "They're going up the ladder to the top of the train! Stop them!"

Grace rushed out of the door in time to see Nat's foot disappear onto the roof of the train. Clarence was nowhere in sight. He must have gone up first. In her dress and high-button boots, she knew climbing would be treacherous. Grace tucked her gun into the holster and bunched the skirt fabric into one hand so she could move up the ladder. Asa would glimpse her ankles and maybe even her calves, but that couldn't be helped — she had to catch the outlaws. Grasping a metal rung overhead, she pulled herself from one rung to the next. Mid-step, one shoe slipped off the rung and she dangled by one arm. Kicking frantically, she felt for a foothold. When she touched another rung, she slid her foot onto it and hugged the ladder with both arms until the thudding of her heart slowed. Gathering up her skirt, she started again, one slow step after another, until she could see over the top of the train.

Half crouching, Nat was moving along the roof of the next carriage. Clarence was one car ahead of him.

"I'll go and get Wyatt," she heard Clarence call. "No sense taking chances."

Grace struggled up another rung. Clinging tightly to the top of the ladder with one hand, she eased her gun out of the holster, then twisted until she could rest her arm on the roof. The hot metal burned through the dress sleeve, but she didn't want to miss. She aimed for Nat's leg, but he took a flying leap onto the roof of the next carriage and her shot went wild. Nat glanced back at the sound of her bullet and whipped out his own pistol.

Grace ducked, and the shot whizzed past overhead. The sudden movement made her foot slip on the rung again, and she wobbled and fought to keep her balance. By the time she was steady and peeking over the top edge once more, Nat was scrambling down the ladder on the side of the passenger car.

But Clarence shouted, "Go back up! They got Sully and Wyatt. We got to get out of here."

Nat clambered back up to the top of the train, but he was bobbing around too much for Grace to get a shot at him.

Then, all of a sudden, the engine rumbled and a huge puff of smoke enveloped them.

She could only make out their forms dimly, but it looked as if they were crawling toward the ladder. With their bodies so low, she couldn't fire accurately. She'd have to wait until they were climbing down the ladder again or until they reached the platform between the carriages below, and she knew getting herself back down the ladder would take longer than continuing forward on top of the train.

Grace tucked her gun into her holster and picked up her skirts. Pulse racing, she crawled onto the train roof. The ground below looked so far away. If she fell . . .

With a sudden jerk, the train started to move.

CHAPTER 26

Grace fell forward, hands outstretched, body flat against the metal. She hugged the roof and prayed she wouldn't slide.

"Grace!" Joe shouted from several carriages down. "Where are you? Are you all right?"

"I'm up on the roof! Get them to stop the train!" she yelled back, but her words were blown away by the wind. She tried again, screaming louder this time. Below her was a figure poised on the platform between the cars, ready to jump. Grace feared letting go of her tentative hold on the speeding train, but she snaked a hand back for her gun. In one swift move, she drew and fired as he jumped. The man groaned as he dropped from the train. It was Clarence. One down, one to go.

Nat was right behind his associate, but before Grace could aim, he ducked back. A few seconds later, just before they passed an area filled with boulders, scrub, and brush, Nat took a flying leap from the train. Grace fired another shot just as the train swayed. Nat cried out and landed hard, clutching his arm. She must have at least nicked him.

Joe called out Grace's name again. "Where are you?"

She screamed. "Up here! Nat jumped from the train. Go after him." By the time she got down the ladder, the other Andersen twin would be long gone.

"What?" Joe cried, shocked.

"Just follow him!" she shouted.

A second later, another figure jumped from the train, curled into a ball, and rolled down the hill. Joe.

Grace eased backward toward the ladder. Her skirts twisted and tangled around her legs, but she forced herself to keep going as the fabric bunched and tore. Keeping her arms curved around the train roof for balance, she felt behind her with her foot for the edge of the roof. But just as she did, with a great screeching of brakes, the train ground to a halt. Grace slid forward then back with the momentum, and when she stopped, her legs dangled over the edge. She hugged the train roof for a few moments, panting. Pulse racing, she finally inched herself down until she touched the first rung. Then, torn and filthy skirts clutched in one hand, she backed down the ladder as fast as she could in her slippery shoes.

When she reached the platform below, she found herself several feet above the sloping ground. She had to help Joe capture Nat. Taking a deep breath, she leaped from the train. One heel caught in the dirt and Grace tumbled down the embankment, scratching herself on rocks, cacti, and sagebrush. Sore and bruised, she picked herself up, dusted off, and limped as fast as she could after the figure racing ahead of her.

Joe zigzagged behind a towering group of rocks and disappeared from sight. Ignoring the pain shooting through her ankle, Grace sped after him. Panting and bleeding from the scratches, she reached the place where Joe had turned off the path, but saw no one.

Then she heard scuffling and grunting coming from behind a nearby set of boulders. Moving as silently as Joe had taught her, Grace inched closer and peered around the nearest boulder. Joe and Nat were wrestling on the ground, both struggling to reach a gun that lay nearby.

"Joe!" Grace shouted. "Get out of the way."

Joe didn't need telling twice. He ducked low and rolled clear. Nat Andersen straightened up and stared at her wide-eyed for a minute. Time seemed to stop as his face floated across her memory, the gang marauding her family's home . . .

That split second of hesitation was all Nat needed. He

reached for his gun, but before he could get off a shot, Grace finally whipped out her own revolver and pulled the trigger. The gun dropped from Nat's hand and he collapsed, but she stood frozen, gun still aimed, fixated on his unmoving form.

Joe's voice came to her as if from a distance.

"Grace?" He edged toward her. Gently, he lowered her arm and pried the gun from her fingers. He slid it into her holster, then embraced her.

"It's over. It's over," he whispered against her hair.

CHAPTER 27

The next morning, Grace woke up stiff and sore. Every muscle ached, but she had one final score to settle. She picked up her hat. Around the crown was the beaded headband the Ndeh had given her. When Cheis presented it to her, it had six eagle feathers, but one feather was already missing. It had fluttered onto Doc Slaughter's body when she'd shot him, and she'd vowed that day to pursue justice until a feather rested on the form of each Guiltless Gang member. One for each member of her family.

Grace headed for the sheriff's office and strode past Sheriff Shaw, Deputy Clayton, and the other guards with only a brief nod. Behind the iron bars of the cell,

Nat Andersen lay on a narrow bed. He'd survived her bullet, barely, and was under medical supervision, although he was not receiving much. Wyatt slumped on the floor beside the bed. Clarence, the two accomplices from the train, and the man who'd guarded the loot that the outlaws had managed to cart off the train also shared the cell.

Grace stepped closer to the bars and pulled two feathers from the band in her hat, rolling them between her fingers. Then she reached a hand into the cell and tossed the first one. It floated through the bars and landed on Nat Andersen's chest. She let the second one go and it fluttered onto Wyatt Andersen's head. He batted at it but missed, and a slight breeze carried it into his lap.

"What the —" Nat began.

"Feathers for cowards. This is justice for the murder of my family — and all the crimes you've perpetrated before and since. You'll swing for what you've done."

With that, Grace turned on her heel and strode off. Three feathers down, three to go.

When she entered the office, Deputy Clayton nudged Sheriff Shaw. "Looks like the best bounty hunter in the West has arrived for her reward."

Shaw laughed. "So the mighty Watkins brothers couldn't handle the job of transporting the fugitive over the state line, eh? You had to come to their rescue?"

It was not the first time Grace had captured bounty for the Watkins brothers, but she just smiled graciously and inclined her head toward both lawmen. "I did what needed to be done. And Joe helped. I couldn't have done it without him."

"Modest as well as skillful. What can I say?" Deputy Clayton reached in his desk drawer and pulled out a small metal box along with a key. "Too much gold here to put in your purse or to walk around town with. Might want to see about depositing most of it in the bank."

Grace nodded. Although she was grateful for the reward and accepted it gladly, her greatest reward was watching those feathers come to rest on two more members of the Guiltless Gang.

And she had special plans for some of this money. It had been heartbreaking to part with Emily once the train reached Fairbank. After promising to take a trip back East to visit Emily and her mother, Grace had stayed aboard the train with Joe for the return trip to Bisbee. The train carried no other passengers except the trussed outlaws, the subdued Watkins brothers, and a group of lawmen from Fairbank.

But Grace promised herself that once she had captured the rest of the Guiltless Gang, she'd make that trip East and present Emily with her share of the reward money. Joe deserved some too.

"Guess we don't need these any longer." Deputy Clayton stepped over to the wanted posters on the wall. He ripped six of them down and tore them to shreds.

"Only three more Guiltless Gang members to go," Grace pointed out. "And I intend to capture them all."

Deputy Clayton started to protest, but Sheriff Shaw cut him off. "We'd be mighty obliged if you would try."

"I'll need your help to track them down. Any idea of the others' whereabouts yet?"

Both men shook their heads. "But the minute we get any clues, Grace, we'll let you know," Sheriff Shaw promised.

When Grace emerged from the sheriff's office, Reverend Byington and Joe stood waiting outside. Joe held the reins of Paint and Bullet, and the preacher hurried over and took Grace's hand. He studied the scratches and bruises on her face with a slight frown, but then smiled. The tenderness in his glance warmed Grace's heart.

"What are you doing here? At the courthouse, I mean," Grace asked the reverend.

"I got a call that one of the train robbers was near death's door. He wanted to confess, so I hurried over."

"Someone confessed?"

Reverend Byington shook his head. "Unfortunately not. As soon as he learned he'd recover, he recanted his story." He sighed. "Sometimes doing God's work can be a huge burden. All these lost souls . . ."

And she was one of the many souls he agonized over, Grace knew.

"But I am grateful for every victory for good," the

preacher went on. "Joe here has been telling me the story of the train robbery. I'm glad to hear that forgiveness and mercy prevailed over the need to seek your own revenge."

Joe gave Grace a sheepish look. "I said you had a chance to shoot Andersen. It even looked like you intended to . . . but then you didn't. I really admire you for that, Grace. Few people would have had that much courage or self-control."

Recalling the blind rage that had overtaken her when she was near Wyatt Andersen, Grace wasn't so sure. Only the thought of Emily watching had stopped her.

Reverend Byington smiled. "I've been praying that God would soften your heart, Grace, and it seems those prayers were answered. Oh, and God answered another one of my prayers too."

He gestured toward the Watkins brothers, waiting in a line near the building exit. Bruised and battered, all four brothers stood stiffly, hats clasped in front of them. Wade's shoulder was wrapped in thick bandages and he winced each time he drew a breath. Beside him, Steven leaned heavily on a cane, his face pale and drawn. Frank's heavily bandaged hand rested in a sling, and Asa stood hunched over, clutching at his back. Grace bit back a smile at their disheveled appearance, and Reverend Byington nodded to each one in turn. "Good afternoon, boys." Then he patted Grace on the shoulder. "I think they have something to say to you. Joe and I'll wait for you here."

The Watkins brothers waited until Grace approached, then Wade said hesitantly, "We, uh, we owe you an apology."

Asa nodded. "If it weren't for you, we might not even be alive." He looked at his brothers for confirmation. One by one they nodded. All except Frank, whose face was pinched in a sour look, but under Asa's scowl Frank gave a barely perceivable nod.

Asa held out a handful of gold coins. "We're right sorry about that other bounty."

Grace brushed the coins away. "Thanks, but I don't need that."

"I don't blame you . . . for being prideful, but . . . the money is . . . rightfully yours." Wade's words were interspersed with deep gasps as he struggled with his breathing.

"I appreciate your offer, but I have more than enough money right here." Grace shook the metal box. It was certainly more than enough money to begin her search for the rest of the Guiltless Gang. Head high, she marched past them to where Joe was waiting.

He grinned at her. "Thought you might like a ride to clear your head." He motioned to the horses he'd already saddled. How had he known that was exactly what she needed? With a grateful glance, Grace mounted Bullet. Because both of them were stiff and sore, they rode slowly out of town and into the hills. They spent the rest of the afternoon letting the horses graze while they rested in the shade of tall boulders and a small stand of trees.

After reminiscing about their parts in the capture of the train robbers, Grace turned to Joe. "Thank you for everything you did to help. I'm glad you were there." She gave him a sly grin. "Guess I did need you after all."

Joe laughed. "Never thought I'd hear you admit that."

Grace gave him a playful swat. "When it's one against five, I might need a little help."

"A little?"

"All right, all right. You were a big help. And so was Emily." Grace shook her head. "But she could have been killed. I'm glad she's on her way back East and away from this notion of bounty hunting."

Joe raised an eyebrow. "To tell you the truth," he admitted, "your bounty hunting still makes me uneasy too."

Grace turned to look at him. "How can I give up now? You've seen the evil this gang is doing. They need to be stopped. I want justice, for everyone around me, and most of all for my family."

Although Joe nodded, he glanced off into the distance with a clenched jaw. Grace couldn't tell what he was thinking. He seemed so remote and far away, and again worrisome thoughts filled her mind. They were tentatively together now, but how long would he wait for her? She was on her way to getting complete justice for her family's murder, and she couldn't stop. No matter if the quest might take her away from the one thing she wanted almost as much . . .

Hoping to close the distance between them, Grace reached for his hand, and Joe grasped it tightly. Then they sat, hand in hand, until the sun sank below the horizon.

ABOUT THE AUTHOR

Erin Johnson grew up watching classic western movies with her father, which fueled her lifelong love of horseback riding. She's always dreamed of being a fierce-talking cowgirl, but writing about one seemed like the next best thing. She loves traveling, painting, riding motorcycles, and teaching. She lives in North Carolina.